THE MARTYR
OF THE
CATACOMBS

THE MARTYR

OF THE

CATACOMBS

A Tale of Ancient Rome

"If after the manner of men I have fought with beasts at Ephesus, what advantageth it me, if the dead rise not?"

(I Cor. 15:32)

MOODY PRESS

CHICAGO

ISBN 0-8024-0011-6

26 27 28 29 30 31 32 Printing/LC/Year 89 88 87 86 85 84

Printed in the United States of America

FOREWORD

An anonymous story entitled, *The Martyr of the Catacombs: A Tale of Ancient Rome,* was published many years ago. A copy of that book was salvaged from an American sailing vessel, commanded by Captain Richard Roberts, abandoned at sea, after a disastrous hurricane in January, 1876. It is now in the possession of his son.

This volume, bearing the same title, is a carefully edited reprint of that book, and it is now jointly sent forth in the hope that it may be used of the Lord to bring vividly before faithful and thoughtful, as well as careless and thoughtless, believers and their children, in these last and evil days, a picture of what the early saints endured for our Lord Jesus Christ, under one of the bitter persecutions of heathen Rome; and which, we believe, will surely be repeated with satanic intensity in the future, under the Roman Empire.

May it remind *us* all that *we may,* if our Lord tarry a while longer in the heavens, be called upon to suffer for His sake.

The Bible no longer has a lawful place in most of our schools and colleges; family prayer is generally a lost habit; our Lord Jesus Christ, God's only begotten and well-beloved Son, is discredited and dishonored in the house of His professed friends; corporate testimony on earth is over; the call to Laodicea to repent is unheeded; and our Lord's promise of communion with Him is now to the individual.

The promise to Smyrna: "Be thou faithful unto death, and I will give thee a crown of life," may reach even unto us of these days.

The blood of the martyrs in Russia and Germany cries from the ground, a warning to Christians of every country.

But we may still send up the longing cry, *"Come, Lord Jesus, come quickly."*

—RICHARD L. ROBERTS

Hartsdale, N. Y.

CONTENTS

CONTENTS

CHAPTER I

THE COLISEUM

Butchered to make a Roman holiday.

IT WAS A GREAT FESTIVAL DAY in Rome. From all quarters vast numbers of people came pouring forth to one common destination. Over the Capitoline Hill, through the Forum, past the Temple of Peace and the Arch of Titus and the imperial palace, on they went till they reached the Coliseum, where they entered its hundred doors and disappeared within.

There a wonderful scene presented itself: below, the vast arena spread out, surrounded by the countless rows of seats which rose to the top of the outer wall, over a hundred feet. The whole extent was covered with human beings of every class and every age. So vast an assemblage gathered in such a way, presenting to view long lines of stern faces, ascending far on high in successive rows, formed a spectacle which has never elsewhere been equaled, and which was calculated beyond all others to awe the soul of the beholder. More than one hundred thousand people were gathered here, animated by one common feeling, and incited by one single passion. It was the thirst for blood which drew them hither, and nowhere can we find a sadder commentary on the boasted civilization of ancient Rome than this her own greatest spectacle.

Here were warriors who had fought in foreign wars and were familiar with deeds of valor, yet they felt no indignation at the scenes of cowardly oppression displayed before them; nobles of ancient families were here, but they could find in these brutal shows no stain upon their country's honor. Philosophers, poets, priests, rulers, the highest as well as the lowest in the land, crowded these seats; but the applauding shout of the patrician was as loud and as eager as that of the plebeian. What hope was there for Rome when the hearts of her people were universally given up to cruelty and brutal oppression?

Upon a raised seat in a conspicuous part of the amphitheater was the Emperor Decius, near whom the chief people among the Romans were gathered. Among these there was a group of officers belonging to the Prætorian guards, who criticized the different points in the scene before them with the air of connoisseurs. Their loud laughter, their gaiety, and their splendid attire made them the object of much attention from their neighbors.

Several preliminary spectacles had been introduced, and now the fights began. Several hand-to-hand combats were presented, most of which resulted fatally, and excited different degrees of interest according to the courage or skill of the combatants. Their effect was to whet the appetite of the spectators to a keener relish, and fill them with eager desire for the more exciting events which were to follow.

One man in particular had drawn down the admiration and applause of the multitude. He was an African from Mauritania, of gigantic strength and stature. But his skill seemed equal to his strength. He wielded his short sword with marvelous dexterity, and thus far had slain every opponent.

He was now matched with a gladiator from Batavia, a man fully equal in stature and strength to himself. The contrast which the two presented was striking. The African was tawny, with glossy curling hair and glittering eyes; the Batavian was light in complexion, with blond hair and keen gray eyes. It was hard to tell which had the advantage, so nearly were they matched in every respect; but as the former had already fought for some time, it was thought that the odds were rather against him. The contest, however, began with great spirit and eagerness on both sides. The Batavian struck tremendous blows, which were parried by the adroitness of the other. The African was quick and furious, but he could do nothing against the cool and wary defense of his vigilant adversary.

At length, at a given signal, the combat was suspended, and the gladiators were led away, not through anything like mercy or admiration, but simply through a shrewd understanding of the best mode of satisfying the Roman public.

It was well understood that they would return again.

Now a large number of men were led into the arena. These were still armed with the short sword. In a moment they had begun the attack. It was not a conflict between two sides, but a general fight, in which every man attacked his neighbor. Such scenes were the most bloody, and therefore the most exciting. A conflict of this kind would always destroy the greatest number in the shortest time. The arena presented a scene of dire confusion. Five hundred armed men in the prime of life and strength all struggled confusedly together. Sometimes they would all be interlocked in one dense mass; at other times they would violently separate into widely scattered individuals, with a heap of dead upon the scene of the combat. But these would assail one another again with undiminished fury; separate combats would spring up all around, the victors in these would rush to take part in others, until at last the survivors had once more congregated in one struggling crowd.

At length their struggles became weaker. Out of five hundred but one hundred remained, and these were wearied and wounded. Suddenly a signal was given, and two men leaped into the arena and rushed from opposite sides upon this crowd. They were the African and the Batavian. Fresh from their repose, they fell upon the exhausted wretches before them, who had neither the spirit to combine nor the strength to resist.

It became a butchery. These two giants slaughtered right and left without mercy, until they alone stood upright upon the arena, and the applause of the innumerable throng came down in thunder to their ears.

These two again attacked each other, and attracted the attention of the spectators while the bodies of the wounded and slain were being removed. The combat was as fierce as before, and precisely similar. The African was agile, the Batavian cautious. But finally the former made a desperate thrust; the Batavian parried it, and returned a stroke like lightning. The African sprang back and dropped his sword. But he was too late, for the stroke of his foe had pierced his left arm. As he fell a roar of joy arose from one hundred thousand human beings. But this was not to be the end, for even while the conqueror stood over his victim the attendants sprang forward and drew him away. Yet the Romans knew, and the wounded man knew that it was not mercy. He was merely to be reserved for a later but a certain fate.

"The Batavian is a skillful fighter, Marcellus," said one young officer to a companion among the group which has been alluded to.

"He is, indeed, Lucullus," replied the other. "I do not think that I ever saw a better gladiator. Indeed, both of them were much better than common."

"They have a better man than either inside there."

"Ah! Who is he?"

"The gladiator Macer. I think he is about the best I have ever seen."

"I have heard of him. Do you think he will be out today?"

"I understood so."

The short conversation was interrupted by a loud roar which came from the vivarium, a place where the wild beasts were confined. It was a fierce and a terrific roar, such as the most savage beasts give when they are at the extremity of hunger and rage.

Soon iron gratings were flung open by men from above, and a tiger stalked forth into the arena. He was from Africa, whence he had been brought but a few days previously. He had been kept three days without food, and his furious rage, which hunger and confinement had heightened to a terrible degree, was awful to behold. Lashing his tail, he walked round the arena gazing with bloodshot eyes upward at the spectators. But their attention was soon diverted to another object. From the opposite side a man was thrust out into the arena. He had no armor, but was naked like all gladiators, with the simple exception of a loincloth. Bearing in his hand the customary short sword, he advanced with a firm pace toward the center of the scene.

All eyes at once were fixed upon this man. "Macer! Macer!" was called around by the innumerable spectators.

The tiger soon saw him, and uttered a short savage growl of fearful import. Macer stood still, with his eyes calmly fixed upon the beast, who, lashing his tail more madly than ever, bounded toward him. Finally the tiger crouched, and then, with one terrific spring, leaped directly upon him. But Macer was prepared. Like a flash he darted to the left, and just as the tiger fell to the earth, he dealt a short, sharp blow straight to his heart. It was a fatal stroke. The huge beast shuddered from head to foot, and drawing all his limbs together, he uttered a last howl that sounded almost like the scream of a human being, and fell dead upon the sand.

Again the applause of the multitude rose like a thunder-peal all around.

"Wonderful!" cried Marcellus. "I never saw skill equal to that of Macer!"

"Without doubt he has been fighting all his life," rejoined his friend.

But soon the carcass of the tiger was drawn away, and again the creak of a grating as it swung apart attracted attention. This time it was a lion. He came forth slowly, and looked all around upon the scene as if in surprise. He was the largest of his species, a giant in size, and had long been preserved for some superior antagonist. He seemed capable of encountering two animals like the tiger that had preceded him. Beside him Macer was like a child.

The lion had fasted long, but he showed no fury like that of the tiger. He walked across the arena, and then completely around it in a kind of trot, as though searching for escape. Finding every side closed, he finally retreated to the center, and putting his face close to the ground, he uttered a roar so deep, so loud, and so long, that the ponderous stones of the Coliseum itself vibrated at the sound.

Macer stood unmoved. Not a muscle of his face changed. He carried his head erect with the same watchful expression, and held his sword ready. At length the lion turned full upon him. The wild beast and the man stood face to face eying one another. But the calm gaze of the man seemed to fill the animal with wrath. He started back with his hair and tail erect and, tossing his mane, he crouched for the dreadful spring.

The vast multitude stood spellbound. Here, indeed, was a sight worthy of their interest.

The dark form of the lion darted forward, but again the form of the gladiator, with his customary maneuver, leaped aside and struck. This time, however, his sword struck a rib, and fell from his hand. The lion was slightly wounded, but the blow served only to rouse his fury to the highest point.

Yet Macer lost not one jot of his coolness in that awful moment. Perfectly unarmed, he stood before the beast waiting his attack. Again and again the lion sprang, but each time he was evaded by the nimble gladiator, who by his own adroit movements contrived to reach the spot where his weapon lay and regain possession of it. Armed with his trusty sword, he waited a final spring. The lion came down as before, but this time Macer's aim was true. The sword pierced his heart. The enormous beast fell, writhing in pain. Rising again to his feet, he

ran across the arena, and with a last roar he fell
dead by the bars at which he had entered.

Macer was now led away, and the Batavian
reappeared. The Romans required variety. A
small tiger was let loose upon the Batavian and
was vanquished. A lion was then set upon him.
He was extremely fierce, although of only ordinary size. It was evident that the Batavian was
not at all equal to Macer. The lion made a
spring and was wounded, but on making a second attack, he caught his opponent and literally
tore him to pieces. Then Macer was sent out
again, and killed this lion easily.

And now, while Macer stood there the recipi-
ent of unbounded applause, a man entered from
the opposite side. It was the African. His arm
had not been bound up, but hung down by his
side covered with blood. He staggered toward
Macer with painful steps. The Romans knew
that he had been sent out to be killed. The
wretch also knew it, for as he drew near to his
antagonist he dropped his sword, and cried out
in a kind of desperation:

"Quick! Kill me, and put me out of pain."

To the amazement of all, Macer stepped back
and flung down his sword. The spectators stared
and wondered. Still more amazed were they
when Macer turned toward the Emperor and
stretched out his hands.

"August Emperor," he cried, "I am a Christian. I will fight wild beasts, but I will not raise
my hand against a fellow man. I can die, but I
will not kill."

Whereupon a mighty murmur arose.

"What does he say?" cried Marcellus. "A Christian! When did that happen?"

"I heard," said Lucullus, "that he was visited in his cell by some of these wretched Christians, and joined their contemptible sect. They are made up of the offscouring of mankind. It is very probable that he is a Christian."

"And will he incur death rather than fight?"

"That is the way with these fanatics."

Rage took the place of surprise in the fierce multitude. They were indignant that a mere gladiator should dare to disappoint them. The attendants rushed out to interfere. The fight must go on. If Macer would not fight he should take the consequences.

But he was firm. Unarmed, he advanced toward the African, whom he could have slain even then with a blow of his fist. The face of the African was like that of a fiend. Surprise, joy, and triumph gleamed in his sinister eyes. Seizing his sword in a firm grasp, he struck Macer to the heart.

"Lord Jesus, receive my spirit—" The words were drowned in a torrent of blood, and this humble but bold witness for Christ passed away from earth to join the noble army of martyrs.

"Are there many such scenes as this?" asked Marcellus.

"Often. Whenever Christians appear. They will fight any number of beasts. Young girls will come firmly to meet lions and tigers, but not one of the madmen will fight with men. The populace are bitterly disappointed in Macer. He is the very best of all the gladiators, and in becoming a Christian he has acted like a fool."

"It must be a wonderful religion which could make a common gladiator act thus," said Marcellus.

"You'll have a chance to learn more about it."

"How so?"

"Haven't you heard? You are appointed to unearth some of these Christians. They have got down in the Catacombs, and they must be hunted up."

"I should think they have enough already. Fifty were burned this morning."

"And a hundred were beheaded last week. But that is nothing. The city is swarming with them. The emperor has determined to restore the old religion perfectly. Since these Christians have appeared, the empire has been declining. He has made up his mind to annihilate them. They are a curse, and must be dealt with accordingly. You will soon understand."[1]

"I haven't been in Rome long enough to know," said Marcellus meekly, "and I do not understand what the Christians really believe. I have heard almost every crime imputed to them. However, if it be as you say, I will have a chance of learning."

But now another scene attracted their attention.

[1] This persecution was by the Emperor Decius, A.D. 249-251, about 2½ years. He was killed in battle with the Goths about the end of A.D. 251.

An old man entered upon the scene. His form was bowed, and his hair silver-white with extreme old age. His appearance was hailed with shouts of derision, although his majestic face and dignified manner were only calculated to excite admiration. As the shouts of laughter and yells of derision came down to his ears, he raised his head and uttered a few words.

"Who is he?" asked Marcellus.

"Alexander, a teacher of the abominable Christian sect. He is so obstinate that he will not recant—"

"Hush, he is speaking."

"Romans!" said the old man. "I am a Christian. My God died for me, and I gladly lay down my life for Him—"

A loud outburst of yells and execrations from the fierce mob drowned his voice. Before it was over three panthers came bounding toward him. He folded his arms, and looking up to Heaven, his lips moved as if murmuring prayers. The savage beasts fell upon him as he stood, and in a few minutes he was torn in pieces.

Other wild animals were now let in. They bounded around the enclosure, they leaped against the barrier, and in their rage assailed one another. It was a hideous scene.

Into the midst of this a band of helpless prisoners was rudely thrust. It was composed chiefly of young girls, who were thus sacrificed to the bloodthirsty passions of the savage Roman mob. The sight would have moved to pity any heart in which all tender feelings had not been blighted.

But pity had no place in Rome. Cowering and fearful, the poor young maidens showed the weakness of human nature when just confronted with death in so terrible a form, but after a few moments faith resumed its power, and raised them above all fear. As the beasts became aware of the presence of their prey and began to draw near, these young maidens joined hands, and raising their eyes to Heaven, sang out a solemn chant which rose clear and wondrously sweet upward to Heaven:

> Unto Him that loved us,
> To Him that washed us from our sins
> In His own blood;
> To Him that made us kings and priests,
> To our God and Father;
> To Him be glory and dominion
> Forever and ever.
> Halleluiah.   Amen!

One by one the voices were hushed in blood, and agony, and death; one by one the shrieks of anguish were mingled with the shouts of praise; and these fair young spirits, so heroic under suffering and faithful unto death, had carried their song to join it with the psalm of the redeemed on high.

CHAPTER II

THE PRÆTORIAN CAMP

*Cornelius the centurion, a just man, and one
that feareth God—*

MARCELLUS WAS BORN in Gades, and had
been brought up in the stern discipline of
a Roman army. He had been quartered in Africa, in Syria, and in Britain, where he had distinguished himself not only by bravery in the
field but also by skill in the camp. For these reasons he had received honors and promotions,
and upon his arrival at Rome, to which place he
had come as the bearer of dispatches, he had so
pleased the emperor that he had been appointed
to an honorable station among the Prætorians.

Lucullus had never been out of Italy, scarcely
indeed out of the city. He belonged to one of the
oldest and noblest Roman families, and enjoyed
corresponding wealth and influence. He was
charmed by the bold and frank nature of Marcellus, and the two young men had become firm
friends. The intimate knowledge of the capital
which Lucullus possessed enabled him also to
be of service to his friend, and the scene which
has been described in the preceding chapter was

one of the first visits which Marcellus had made to the renowned Coliseum.

The Prætorian camp was situated close to the city wall, to which it was joined by another wall which enclosed it The soldiers lived in rooms like cells made in the wall itself. They were a numerous and finely appointed body of men, and their situation at the capital gave them a power and an influence so great that for ages they controlled the government of the capital. A command among the Prætorians was a sure road to fortune, and Marcellus could look forward with well-grounded prospects of future honors.

On the morning of the following day Lucullus entered his room. After the usual salutation he spoke of the fight which they had witnessed.

"Such scenes are not to my taste," said Marcellus. "They are cowardly. I like to see two well-trained men engage in a fair combat, but such butchery as you have in the Coliseum is detestable. Why should Macer be murdered? He was a brave man, and I honor his courage. And why should old men and young children be handed over to wild beasts?"

"It is the law. They are Christians."

"That is always the answer. What have the Christians done? I have seen them in all parts of the world, but have never known them to be engaged in disturbances."

"They are the worst of mankind."

"So it is said; but what proof is there?"

"Proof? It is too well known. Their crime is

that they plot in secret against the laws and the religion of the State. So intense is the hatred which they bear toward our institutions that they will die rather than offer sacrifice. They own no king or monarch but the crucified Jew who they believe is alive now. And they show their malevolence to us by asserting that we shall all hereafter be tortured in Hades forever."

"This may be true. I know not. I know nothing at all about them."

"The city is swarming with them; the empire is overrun. And mark this. The decline of our empire, which all see and lament, the spread of weakness and insubordination, the contraction of our boundaries—all this increases as the Christians increase. To what else are these evils owing if not to them?"

"How have they produced this?"

"By their detestable teachings and practices. They teach that fighting is wrong, that soldiers are the basest of men, that our glorious religion under which we have prospered is a curse, and that the immortal gods are accursed demons. In their teachings they aim to overthrow all morality. In their private practices they perform the darkest and foulest crimes. They always keep by themselves in impenetrable secrecy, but sometimes we overhear their evil discourses and lewd songs."

"All this is indeed serious, and if true, they deserve severe punishment. But according to your own statement they keep by themselves, and but little is known of them. Tell me, did those who suffered yesterday seem like this? Did that old man look as though he had passed his life in vicious scenes? Did those fair young girls sing lewd songs as they waited for the lions?"

Unto Him that loved us;
To Him that washed us from our sins.

And Marcellus sang in a soft voice the words which he had heard.

"I confess, my friend, that I mourned for them."

"And I," said Marcellus, "could have wept had I not been a Roman soldier. Consider for a moment. You tell me things about these Christians which you confess only to have learned from those who themselves are ignorant. You assert that they are infamous and base, the off-scouring of the earth. I see them confronted with a death that tries the highest qualities of the soul. They meet it nobly. They die grandly. In all her history Rome can produce no greater scene of devotion than that of yesterday. You say they detest soldiers, yet they are brave; you tell me that they are traitors, yet they do not resist the laws; you declare that they are impure, yet if purity is on earth, it belonged to those maidens who died yesterday."

"You are enthusiastic for those outcasts."

"Not so, Lucullus. I wish to know the truth. All my life I have heard these reports. But yesterday for the first time I suspected that they might be false. I now question you earnestly, and I find that your knowledge is based upon nothing. I now remember that throughout all the world these Christians are peaceable and honest. They are engaged in no riots or disturbances, and none of these crimes with which they are charged can be proved against them. Why, then, should they die?"

"The emperor has good reasons no doubt for his course."

"He may be instigated by ignorant or malicious advisers."

"I think it is entirely his own design."

"The number of those that have been put to death is very large."

"Oh, yes, some thousands; but plenty more remain; these, however, are out of reach. And that reminds me of my errand here. I bring you the imperial commission."

Lucullus drew from the folds of his military mantle a scroll of parchment, which he handed to Marcellus. The latter eagerly examined its contents. It appointed him to a higher grade, and commissioned him to search out and arrest the Christians in their hiding places, mentioning particularly the Catacombs.

Marcellus read it with a clouded brow, and laid it down.

"You do not seem very glad."

"I confess the task is unpleasant. I am a soldier, and do not like to hunt out old men and weak children for the executioner; yet as a soldier I must obey. Tell me something about these Catacombs."

"The Catacombs? It is a subterranean district that extends to unknown bounds underneath the city. The Christians fly to the Catacombs whenever there is danger, and they also are in the habit of burying their dead there. Once there, they are beyond the reach of the utmost powers of the State."

"Who made the Catacombs?"

"No one knows exactly. They have existed for ages. I believe that they were excavated for the sake of getting building sand for cement. At present all our cement comes from there, and you may see workmen bringing it into the city along any of the great roads. They have to go far away for it now, for in the course of ages they have excavated so much beneath us that this city now rests upon a foundation like a honeycomb."

"Is there any regular entrance?"

"There are innumerable entrances. That is the difficulty. If there were but few, then we might catch the fugitives. But we cannot tell from which direction to advance upon them."

"Is any district suspected?"

"Yes. About two miles down the Appian Way, near the tomb of Cæcilia Metella, the large round tower, you know, bodies have frequently been discovered. It is conjectured that these are the bodies of the Christians which have been obtained from the amphitheater and carried away for burial. On the approach of the guards, the Christians have dropped the bodies and fled. But, after all, this gives no assistance, for after you enter the Catacombs you are no nearer your aim than before. No human being can penetrate that infinite labyrinth without assistance from those who live there."

"Who live there?"

"The fossors, who still excavate sand for the builders. They are nearly all Christians, and are always at work cutting out graves for the dead of the Christians. These men have lived there all their lives, and are not only familiar with the passages, but they have a kind of instinct to guide them."

"Were you ever in the Catacombs?"

"Once, long ago, a fossor guided me. I remained but a short time. My impression was that it was the most terrible place in all the world."

"I have heard of the Catacombs, but never before knew anything about them. It is strange that they are so little known. Could not these fossors be engaged to lead the guards through this labyrinth?"

"No. They will not betray the Christians."

"Have they been tried?"

"Certainly. Some comply, and lead the officers of justice through a network of passages till they get bewildered. Their torches become extinguished, and they grow terrified. Then they ask to be led back. The fossor declares that the Christians must have fled, and so takes back the soldiers to the starting point."

"Are none resolute enough to continue on till they find the Christians?"

"If they insist upon continuing the search, the fossor will lead them on forever. But he merely leads them through the countless passages which intersect some particular district."

"Are none found who will actually betray the fugitives?"

"Sometimes; but of what use is it? Upon the first alarm, every Christian vanishes through the side ways, which open everywhere."

"My prospect of success seems small."

"Very small, but much is hoped from your boldness and shrewdness. If you succeed in this enterprise it will be your fortune. And now, farewell. You have learned from me all that I know. You will find no difficulty in learning more from any one of the fossors."

So saying, Lucullus departed.

Marcellus leaned his head on his hands, and lost himself in thought. But ever amid his meditations came floating the strains of that glorious melody which told of triumph over death:

> Unto Him that loved us,
> To Him that washed us from our sins.

CHAPTER III

THE APPIAN WAY

Sepulchers in sad array
Guard the ashes of the mighty
Slumbering on the Appian Way.

MARCELLUS ENTERED upon the duty that lay before him without delay. Upon the following day he set out upon his investigations. It was merely a journey of inquiry, so he took no soldiers with him. Starting forth from the Prætorian Barracks, he walked out of the city and down the Appian Way.

This famous road was lined on both sides with magnificent tombs, all of which were carefully preserved by the families to whom they belonged. Farther back from the road lay houses and villas as thickly clustered as in the city. The open country was a long distance away.

At length he reached a huge round tower, which stood about two miles from the gate. It was built with enormous blocks of travertine, and ornamented beautifully yet simply. Its severe style and solid construction gave it an air of bold defiance against the ravages of time.

At this point Marcellus paused and looked

back. To a stranger in Rome, every view presented something new and interesting. Most remarkable was the long line of tombs. There were the last resting places of the great, the noble, and the brave of elder days, whose epitaphs announced their claims to honor on earth, and their dim prospects in the unknown life to come. Art and wealth had reared these sumptuous monuments, and the pious affection of ages had preserved them from decay. Here where he stood was the sublime mausoleum of Cæcilia Metella; farther away were the tombs of Calatinus and the Servilii. Still farther his eye fell upon the resting place of the Scipios, the classic architecture of which was hallowed by "the dust of its heroic dwellers."

The words of Cicero recurred to his mind, "When you go out of the Porta Capena, and see the tombs of Calatinus, of the Scipios, the Servilii, and the Metelli, can you consider that the buried inmates are unhappy?"

There was the arch of Drusus spanning the road; on one side was the historic grotto of Egeria, and farther on the spot where Hannibal once stood and hurled his javelin at the walls of Rome. The long lines of tombs went on till in the distance they were terminated by the lofty pyramid of Caius Cestius, and the whole presented the grandest scene of sepulchral magnificence that could be found on earth.

On every side the habitations of men covered the ground, for the Imperial City had long ago burst the bounds that originally confined it, and sent its houses far away on every side into the country, till the traveler could scarcely tell where the country ended and where the city began.

From afar the deep hum of the city, the roll of innumerable chariots, and the multitudinous tread of its many feet greeted his ears. Before him rose monuments and temples, the white sheen of the imperial palace, the innumerable domes and columns towering upward like a city in the air, and high above all the lofty Capitoline mount, crowned with the shrine of Jove.

But more impressive than all the splendor of the home of the living was the solemnity of the city of the dead.

What an array of architectural glory was displayed around him! There arose the proud monuments of the grand old families of Rome. Heroism, genius, valor, pride, wealth, everything that man esteems or admires, here animated the eloquent stone and awakened emotion. Here were the visible forms of the highest influences of the old pagan religion. Yet their effects upon the soul never corresponded with the splendor of their outward forms, or the pomp of their ritual. The epitaphs of the dead showed not faith, but love of life, triumphant; not the assurance of immortal life, but a sad longing after the pleasures of the world.

Such were the thoughts of Marcellus as he mused upon the scene and again recalled the words of Cicero, "Can you think that the buried inmates are unhappy?"

"These Christians," thought he, "whom I am

now seeking, seem to have learned more than I can find in all our philosophy. They not only have conquered the fear of death, but have learned to die rejoicing. What secret power have they which can thus inspire even the youngest and the feeblest among them? What is the hidden meaning of their song? My religion can only hope that I may not be unhappy; theirs leads them to death with triumphant songs of joy."

But how was he to prosecute his search after the Christians? Crowds of people passed by, but he saw none who seemed capable of assisting him. Buildings of all sizes, walls, tombs, and temples were all around, but he saw no place that seemed at all connected with the Catacombs. He was quite at a loss what to do.

He went down into the street and walked slowly along, carefully scrutinizing every person whom he met, and examining closely every building. Yet no result was obtained from this beyond the discovery that the outward appearance gave no sign of any connection with subterranean abodes. The day passed on, and it grew late; but Marcellus remembered that there were many entrances to the Catacombs, and still he continued his search, hoping before the close of the day to find some clue

At length his search was rewarded. He had walked backward and forward and in every direction. often retracing his steps and returning many times to the place of starting. Twilight was coming on, and the sun was near the edge of the horizon, when his quick eye caught sight of a man who was walking in an opposite direction, followed by a boy. The man was dressed in coarse apparel, stained and damp with sand and earth. His complexion was blanched and pallid, like that of one who has long been imprisoned, and his whole appearance at once arrested the glance of the young soldier.

He stepped up to him, and laying his hand upon his shoulder said:

"You are a fossor. Come with me."

The man looked up. He saw a stern face. The sight of the officer's dress terrified him. In an instant he darted away, and before Marcellus could turn to follow, he had rushed into a side lane and was out of sight.

But Marcellus secured the boy.

"Come with me," said he.

The poor lad looked up with such an agony of fear that Marcellus was moved.

"Have mercy, for my mother's sake; she will die if I am taken."

The boy fell at his feet murmuring this in broken tones.

"I will not hurt you. Come," and he led him away toward an open space out of the way of the passers-by.

"Now," said he, stopping and confronting the boy, "tell me the truth. Who are you?"

"My name is Pollio," said the boy.

"Where do you live?"

"In Rome."

"What are you doing here?"

"I was out on an errand."

"Who was that man?"

"A fossor."

"What were you doing with him?"

"He was carrying a bundle for me."

"What was in the bundle?"

"Provisions."

"To whom were you carrying it?"

"To a destitute person out here."

"Where does he live?"

"Not far from here."

"Now, boy, tell me the truth. Do you know anything about the Catacombs?"

"I have heard about them," said the boy quietly.

"Were you ever in them?"

"I have been in some of them."

"Do you know anybody who lives in them?"

"Some people. The fossor stays there."

"You were going to the Catacombs then with him?"

"What business would I have there at such a time as this?" said the boy innocently.

"That is what I want to know. Were you going there?"

"How would I dare to go there when it is forbidden by the laws?"

"It is now evening," said Marcellus abruptly, "come with me to the evening service at yonder temple."

The boy hesitated. "I am in a hurry," said he.

"But you are my prisoner. I never neglect the worship of the gods. You must come and assist me at my devotions."

"I cannot," said the boy firmly.

"Why not?"

"I am a Christian."

"I knew it. And you have friends in the Catacombs, and you are going there now. They are the destitute people to whom you are carrying provisions, and the errand on which you are is for them."

The boy held down his head and was silent.

"I want you now to take me to the entrance of the Catacombs."

"Oh, generous soldier, have mercy! Do not ask me that. I cannot do it! I will not betray my friends."

"You need not. It is nothing to show the entrance among the many thousands that lead down below. Do you think that the guards do not know every one?"

The boy thought for a moment, and at length signified his assent.

Marcellus took his hand and followed his lead. The boy turned away to the right of the Appian Way, walking a short distance. Here he came to an uninhabited house. He entered, and went down into the cellar. There was a door which apparently opened into a closet. The boy pointed to this, and stopped.

"I wish to go down," said Marcellus, firmly.

"You would not dare to go down alone surely; would you?"

"The Christians say that they do not commit murder. Why then should I fear? Lead on."

"I have no torches."

"But I have some. I came prepared. Go on."

"I cannot."

"Do you refuse?"

"I must refuse," said the boy. "My friends and my relatives are below. Sooner than lead you to them I would die a hundred deaths."

"You are bold. You do not know what death is."

"Do I not? What Christian can fear death? I have seen many of my friends die in agony, and I have helped to bury them. I will not lead you there. Take me away to prison."

The boy turned away.

"But if I take you away what will your friends think? Have you a mother?"

The boy bowed his head and burst into a passion of tears. The mention of that dear name had overcome him.

"I see that you have, and that you love her. Lead me down, and you shall join her again."

"I will never betray them. I will die first. Do with me as you wish."

"If I had any evil intentions," said Marcellus, "do you think I would go down unaccompanied?"

"What can a soldier, and a Prætorian, want with the persecuted Christians if not to destroy them?"

"Boy, I have no evil intentions. If you guide me down below, I swear I will not use my knowledge against your friends. When I am below, I will be a prisoner, and they can do with me what they like."

"Do you swear that you will not betray them?"

"I do, by the life of Cæsar and the immortal gods," said Marcellus, solemnly.

"Come along, then," said the boy. "We do not need torches. Follow me carefully."

And the lad entered the narrow opening.

CHAPTER IV

THE CATACOMBS

No light, but rather darkness visible
Served only to discover sights of woe,
Regions of sorrow, doleful shades.

THEY WENT ON in utter darkness, until at
length the passage widened and they came
to steps which led below. Marcellus held the
boy's dress and followed him.

It was certainly a situation that might pro-
voke alarm. He was voluntarily placing himself
in the power of men whom his class had driven
from the upper air into these drear abodes. To
them he could only be known as a persecutor.
Yet such was the impression which he had
formed of their gentleness and meekness that
he had no fear of harm. It was in the power of
this boy to lead him to death in the thick darkness of these impenetrable labyrinths, but even
of this he did not think. It was a desire to know
more of these Christians, to get at their secret,
that led him on, and as he had sworn, so had he
resolved that this visit should not be made use
of to their betrayal or injury.

After descending for some time, they walked
along the level ground. Soon they turned and

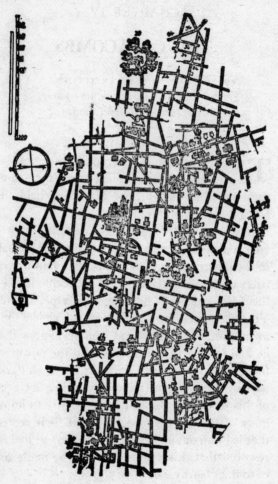

PLAN OF THE CATACOMBS.

entered a small vaulted chamber which was lighted from the faint glow of a furnace. The boy had walked on with the unhesitating step of one perfectly familiar with the way. Arriving at the chamber, he lighted a torch which lay on the floor and resumed his journey.

There is something in the air of a burial place which is unlike that of any other place. It is not altogether the closeness, or the damp, or the sickening smell of earth, but a certain subtle influence which unites with them and intensifies them. The spell of the dead is there, and it rests alike on mind and body. Such was the air of the Catacombs. Cold and damp, it struck upon the visitor like the chill atmosphere from the realms of death. The living felt the mysterious power of death.

The boy Pollio went on before and Marcellus followed after. The torch but faintly illumined the intense darkness. No beam of day, no ray however weak, could ever enter here to relieve the thickness of the oppressive gloom. It was literally darkness that might be felt. The torch-light shone out but a few paces and then died in the darkness.

The path went winding on with innumerable turnings. Suddenly Pollio stopped and pointed downward. Peering through the gloom, Marcellus saw an opening in the path which led farther down. It was a pit to which no bottom appeared.

"Where does this lead to?"

"Below."

"Are there more passages below?"

"Oh, yes. As many as there are here, and still below that again. I have been in three different stories of these paths, and some of the old fossors say that in certain places they go down to a very great depth."

The passage wound along till all idea of locality was utterly lost. Marcellus could not tell whether he was within a few paces of the entrance or many furlongs off. His bewildered thoughts soon began to turn to other things. As the first impressions of gloom departed, he looked more particularly upon what he passed, and regarded more closely the many wonders of this strange place. All along the walls were tablets which appeared to cover long and narrow excavations. These cellular niches were ranged on both sides so closely that but little space was left between. The inscriptions that were upon the tablets showed that they were Christian tombs. He had not time to stop and read, but he noticed the frequent recurrence of the same expression, such as:

HONORIA—SHE SLEEPS IN PEACE

FAUSTA—IN PEACE

On nearly every tablet he saw the same sweet, gentle word. "PEACE," thought Marcellus; "what wonderful people are these Christians, who even amid such scenes as these can cherish their lofty contempt of death!"

His eyes grew more and more accustomed to the gloom as he walked along. Now the passage way grew narrower; the roof drooped, the sides approached; they had to stoop and go along more slowly. The walls were rough and rudely cut as the workmen left them when they drew along here their last load of sand for the edifices above. Subterranean damps and fungus growths overspread them in places, deepening their somber color and filling the air with thick moisture, while the smoke of the torches made the atmosphere still more oppressive.

They passed hundreds of side passages and scores of places where many paths met, all branching off in different directions. These innumerable paths showed Marcellus how hopelessly he was now cut off from the world above. This boy held his life in his hands.

"Do any ever lose their way?"

"Often."

"What becomes of them?"

"Sometimes they wander till they meet some friends, sometimes they are never heard of again. But at present, most of us know the place so well that if we lose our way we soon wander into familiar paths again."

One thing particularly struck the young soldier, and that was the immense preponderance of small tombs. Pollio told him that they were those of children, and thus opened to him thoughts and emotions unfelt before.

"Children!" thought he. "What do they here, the young, the pure, the innocent? Why were they not buried above, where the sun might shine kindly and the flowers bloom sweetly over

their graves? Did they tread such dark paths as
these on their way through life? Did they bear
their part in the sufferings of those that lin-
gered here fleeing from persecution? Did the
noxious air and the never-ending gloom of these
drear abodes shorten their fair young lives, and
send their stainless spirits out of life before their
time?"

"We have been a long time on the way," said
Marcellus, "will we soon be there?"

"Very soon," said the boy.

Whatever ideas Marcellus might have had
about hunting out these fugitives before he entered here, he now saw that all attempts to do
so must be in vain. An army of men might enter here and never come in sight of the Christians. The farther they went, the more hopeless
would be their journey. They could be scattered
through the innumerable passages and wander
about till they died.

But now a low sound arose from afar which
arrested his attention. Sweet beyond all descrip-
tion, low and musical, it came down the long
passages and broke upon his charmed senses like
a voice from the skies.

As they went on, a light beamed before them
which cast forth its rays into the darkness. The
sounds grew louder, now swelling into a magnificent chorus, now dying away into a tender
wail of supplication.

In a few minutes they reached a turn in the
path, and then a scene burst upon their sight.

"Stop," said Pollio, arresting his companion

and extinguishing the torch. Marcellus obeyed, and looked earnestly at the spectacle before him. It was a vaulted chamber about fifteen feet in height and thirty feet square. In this place there were crowded about a hundred people, men, women, and children. At one side there was a table, behind which stood a venerable man who appeared to be the leader among them. The place was illuminated with the glare of torches which threw a lurid glow upon the assembly. The people were careworn and emaciated, and their faces were characterized by the same pallor which Marcellus had observed in the fossor. But the expression which now rested upon them was not of sorrow, or misery, or despair. Hope illuminated their eyes, their upturned faces spoke of joy and triumph. The scene moved the soul of the beholder to its inmost depths, for it confirmed all that he had seen of the Christians, their heroism, their hope, their peace, which rested on something hidden from him. As he listened he heard their song, chanted by the whole congregation:

Great and marvelous are Thy works,
    Lord God Almighty.
Just and true are Thy ways,
    Thou King of saints.
Who shall not fear Thee, O Lord, and glorify
    Thy name?
    For Thou only art holy.
For all nations shall come and worship before
    Thee,
For Thy judgments are made manifest.

Then there was a pause. The venerable leader read something from a scroll which was new to Marcellus. It was a sublime assertion of the immortality of the soul, and life after death. The congregation seemed to hang upon the words as though they were the words of life. Finally, the reader came to a burst of joyous exclamation which drew murmurs of gratitude and enthusiastic hope from the audience. The words thrilled upon the heart of the listener, though he did not understand their full meaning: "O death, where is thy sting? O grave, where is thy victory? The sting of death is sin; and the strength of sin is the law. But thanks be to God, which giveth us the victory, through our Lord Jesus Christ."

These words seemed to open to his mind a new world with new thoughts. Sin, death, Christ, with all the infinite train of ideas that rested upon them, arose dimly before his awakening soul. The desire for the Christian's secret which he had conceived now burned more eagerly within him.

The leader raised his head, and stretching out his hands, uttered a fervent prayer. Addressing the invisible God, he poured forth a confession of unworthiness, and gave thanks for cleansing from sin through the atoning blood of Christ. He prayed that the Spirit from on high might so work within that they would become holy. Then he enumerated their sorrows, and prayed for deliverance, asking for faith in life, victory in death, and abundant entrance into Heaven for the sake of the Redeemer, Jesus.

After this followed another chant which was sung as before:

Behold, the tabernacle of God is with men,
And He will dwell with them,
And they shall be His people,
And God Himself shall be with them
And be their God.
And God shall wipe away all tears from their eyes,
And there shall be no more death, nor sorrow, nor sighing,
Neither shall there be any more pain,
For the former things are passed away.   Amen.
Blessing, and glory, and wisdom,
And thanksgiving, and honor, and power, and might,
Be unto our God
Forever and ever.   Amen.

Now the congregation began to disperse. Pollio walked forward, leading Marcellus. At the sight of his martial figure and glittering armor they all started backward, and would have fled by the different paths. But Marcellus called in a loud voice:

"Fear not, Christians, I am alone and in your power."

Upon this they all turned back, and looked at him with anxious curiosity. The aged man who led the meeting advanced and looked earnestly upon him.

"Who are you, and why do you seek us out in the last resting place that is left to us on earth?"

"Do not suspect me of evil. I come alone, unattended. I am at your mercy."

"But what can a soldier and a Prætorian wish of us? Are you pursued? Are you a criminal? Is your life in danger?"

"No. I am an officer high in rank and authority. But I have all my life been seeking anxiously after the truth. I have heard much of you Christians, but in these times of persecution it is difficult to find you in Rome. I have sought you here."

At this the aged man requested the assembly to withdraw, that he might converse with the newcomer. The others readily did so, and retired by different ways, feeling much relieved. A pale lady advanced eagerly to Pollio and caught him in her arms.

"How long you were, my son!"

"I encountered this officer, dear Mother, and was detained."

"Thank God, you are safe. But who is he?"

"I think he is an honest man," said the boy, "see how he confides in us."

"Cæcilia," said the leader, "do not go away for a little time." The lady remained, and a few others did the same.

"I am Honorius," said the old man, addressing Marcellus, "a humble elder in the Church of Christ. I believe that you are sincere and earnest. Tell us now what you want with us."

"My name is Marcellus, and I am a captain in the Prætorian Guard."

"Alas!" cried Honorius, and clasping his hands he fell back in his seat. The others looked at Marcellus with mournful eyes, and the Lady Cæcilia cried out in an agony of grief,

"O Pollio! How have you betrayed us!"

CHAPTER V

THE CHRISTIAN'S SECRET

The mystery of godliness, God manifest
in the flesh.

THE YOUNG SOLDIER stood astonished at the effect which his name produced.

"Why do you all tremble so?" said he. "Is it on my account?"

"Alas!" said Honorius. "Though we are banished to this place, we have constant communication with the city. We have heard that new efforts were to be made to persecute us more severely, and that Marcellus, a captain in the Prætorians, had been appointed to search us out. We see you here among us, our chief enemy. Have we not cause to fear? Why should you track us here?"

"You have no cause to fear me," cried Marcellus, "even if I were your worst enemy. Am I not in your power? If you choose to detain me, could I escape? If you killed me, could I resist? I am helpless among you. My situation here, alone among you, is proof that there is no danger from me."

"True," said Honorius, resuming his calm demeanor; "you are right; you could never return without our assistance."

"Hear me, then, and I will explain all to you. I am a Roman soldier. I was born in Spain, and was brought up in virtue and morality. I was taught to fear the gods and do my duty. I have been in many lands, and have confined myself chiefly to my profession. Yet I have never neglected religion. In my chamber I have studied all the writings of the philosophers of Greece and Rome. The result is that I have learned from them to despise our gods and goddesses, who are no better, and even worse than myself.

"From Plato and Cicero I learn that there is one Supreme Deity whom it is my duty to obey. But how can I know Him, and how shall I obey Him? I learn, too, that I am immortal, and shall become a spirit when I die. How shall I be then? Shall I be happy or miserable? How shall I secure happiness in that spiritual life? They describe the glories of that immortal life in eloquent language, but they give no directions for common men like me. To learn more of this is the desire of my soul.

"The priests can tell me nothing. They are wedded to old forms and ceremonies in which they do not believe. The old religion is dead, and men care for it no more.

"In different lands I have heard much of Christians. Shut up in the camp, I have not had much opportunity to see them. Indeed, I never cared to know them until lately. I have heard all the usual reports about their immorality, their secret vice, their treasonable doctrines. I believed all this until lately.

"A few days ago I was in the Coliseum. There, first, I learned something about the Christians. I saw the gladiator Macer, a man to whom fear was utterly unknown, lay down his life calmly rather than do what he believed to be wrong. I saw an old man meet death with a peaceful smile; and above all, I saw a band of young girls give themselves up to the wild beasts with a song of triumph on their lips:

> Unto Him that loved us,
> That washed us from our sins."

As Marcellus spoke a wonderful effect was produced. The eyes of his listeners glistened with eagerness and joy. When he mentioned Macer, they looked at each other with meaning glances; when he spoke of the old man, Honorius bowed his head; and when he spoke of the children and murmured the words of their song, they turned away their faces and wept.

"For the first time in my life I saw death conquered. I myself can meet death without terror, and so can every soldier when he comes to it in the battlefield. It is our profession. But these people rejoiced in death. Here were not soldiers, but children, who carried the same wonderful feeling in their hearts.

"Since then I have thought of nothing else. Who is He that loved you? Who is He that washes you from your sins? Who is He that causes this sublime courage and hope to arise within you? What is it that supports you here?

Who is He to whom you were just now praying?

"I have a commission to lead soldiers against you and destroy you. But I wish to learn more of you first. And I swear by the Supreme that my present visit shall bring no harm to you. Tell me, then, the Christian's secret."

"Your words," said Honorius, "are true and sincere. Now I know that you are no spy or enemy, but an inquiring soul sent here by the Spirit to learn that which you have long been seeking. Rejoice, for he that cometh unto Christ shall be in no wise cast out.

"You see before you men and women who have left friends, and home, and honor, and wealth, to live here in want, and fear, and sorrow, and they count all this as nothing for Christ; yes, they count even their own lives nothing. They give up all for Him who loved them.

"You are right, Marcellus, in thinking that there is some great power which can do all this. It is not fanaticism, nor delusion, nor excitement. It is the knowledge of the truth and love for the living God.

"What you have sought for all your life is our dearest possession. Treasured up in our hearts, it is worth far more to us than all that the world can give. It gives us happiness in life even in this place of gloom, and in death it makes us victorious.

"You wish to know the Supreme Being. Our

faith (Christianity) is His revelation, and through this He makes Himself known. Infinite in greatness and power, He also is infinite in love and mercy. This faith draws us so closely to Him that He is our best friend, our guide, our comfort, our hope, our all, our Creator, our Redeemer, and our present and final Saviour.

"You wish to know of the immortal life. Our Scriptures tell of this. They show us that believing in Jesus Christ the Son of God, and loving and serving God on earth, we shall dwell with Him in infinite eternal blessedness in Heaven. They show us how to live so as to please Him here, and make us know how we shall praise Him hereafter. By them we learn that death, though our enemy, is no longer a curse to the believer, but rather a blessing, since 'to depart and be with Christ is far better' than to remain here, for we enter into the presence of Him 'who loved us and gave himself for us.' "

"Oh, then," cried Marcellus, "if this be so, make known to me this truth. For this I have looked for years; for this I have prayed to that Supreme Being of whom I have heard. You are the possessor of that which I long to know. The end and aim of my life lies here. The whole night is before us. Do not put me off, but at once tell me all. Has the true God, indeed, made known all this, and have I been ignorant of it?"

Tears of joy glistened in the eyes of the Christians. Honorius murmured a few words of silent thankfulness and prayer. After which he drew forth a manuscript, which he handled with tender care.

"Here," said he, "beloved youth, is the word of life which came from God, which brings such peace and joy to man. In this we find all that the soul desires. In these divine words we learn that which can be found nowhere else; and though the mind may brood over it for a lifetime, yet the extent of its glorious truths can never be reached."

Then Honorius opened the Book and began to tell Marcellus of Jesus. He told him of the promise in Eden of One who would bruise Satan's head, of the long succession of prophets which had heralded His coming; of the chosen people through whom God had kept alive the knowledge of the truth for so many ages, and of the marvelous works which they had witnessed. He read of the announcement of the Son of God to be born of the virgin. He read of His birth; His childhood; His first appearance; His miracles; His teachings. All this he read, with a few comments of his own, from the sacred manuscript.

Then he related the treatment which He received; the scorn, contempt, and persecution which hurried Him on to His betrayal and condemnation.

Finally, he read the account of His death on the cross on Calvary.

Upon Marcellus the effect of all this was wonderful. Light seemed to burst upon his mind. The holiness of God, which turned with abhorrence from human sin; His justice, which demanded punishment; His patience, which endured so much; His mercy, which contrived a way to save His creatures from the ruin which they have drawn on themselves; His amazing love, which gave His only begotten and beloved Son; the love which brought Him down to sacrifice Himself for their salvation, all were clear. When Honorius reached the end of the mournful story of Calvary, and came to the cry: "My God, my God, why hast thou forsaken me?" followed by the triumphant cry, "It is finished!" he was roused by a sob from Marcellus. Looking up through the tears which dimmed his own eyes, he saw the form of the strong man bowed, and his frame quivering with emotion.

"No more, no more now," he murmured. "Let me think of Him:

> Him who loved us,
> Who washed us from our sins,
> In His own blood."

And Marcellus buried his face in his hands.

Honorius raised his eyes to Heaven and prayed. The two were alone, for their companions had quietly departed. The light from a lamp in a niche behind Honorius but dimly illumined the scene. Thus they remained in silence for a long time.

At last Marcellus raised his head.

"I feel," said he, "that I too had a part in

causing the death of the Holy One. Read on, more of that word of life, for my own life hangs upon it."

Then Honorius read again the account of the crucifixion and the burial of Jesus; the resurrection on the morning of the third day, and the ascension to the right hand of God. He read of the descent of the Holy Spirit on the day of Pentecost, baptizing believers into one Body; of His abiding presence, making the body of the believer His temple; and of His wonderful ministry, glorifying Christ, and revealing Christ to repentant sinners.

Nor did he end with this, but sought to bring peace to the soul of Marcellus, reading to him the words of Jesus which invite the sinner to come to Him, and assure him of eternal life as a present possession the moment he accepts Him as Lord and Saviour. He read of the "new birth," the new life, and the promises of Jesus to come again and catch up His blood-washed people to meet Him in the air.

"It is the Word of God," cried Marcellus. "It is a voice from Heaven. My heart responds to everything that I have heard, and I know that it must be eternal truth! But how can I become possessed of this salvation? My eyes seem now to be cleared of mist. I know myself at last. Before, I thought I was a just and a righteous man. But beside the Holy One, of whom I now have learned, I sink down into the dust; I see that I am a criminal before Him, guilty and lost. How can I be saved?"

"Christ Jesus came into the world to seek and save the lost."

"Oh, how may I receive Him?"

" 'The word is nigh thee, even in thy mouth, and in thy heart: that is, the word of faith, which we preach; that if thou shalt confess with thy mouth the Lord Jesus, and shalt believe in thine heart that God hath raised him from the dead, thou shalt be saved. For with the heart man believeth unto righteousness; and with the mouth confession is made unto salvation.' "

"But is there nothing I must do?"

" 'By grace are ye saved through faith; and that [salvation] not of yourselves: it is the gift of God: not of works, lest any man should boast.' 'The *wages* of sin is death; but the *gift* of God is eternal life through Jesus Christ our Lord.' "

"But is there no sacrifice I can offer?"

"He has offered one sacrifice for sins forever, and is now set down at the right hand of God. He is able to save forevermore all who come 'unto God by him, seeing he ever liveth to make intercession for them.' "

"Oh, then, if I may dare approach, teach me the words, lead me to Him!"

In the dimness of that gloomy vault, in the solitude and solemn silence, Honorius knelt down, and Marcellus bowed himself beside him. The venerable Christian raised his voice in prayer. Marcellus felt that his own soul was being lifted up to Heaven, to the very presence of the Saviour, by the power of that fervent, believing prayer. The words found echo in his own soul and spirit; and in his deep abasement, he rested his need upon his companion, so that he might present it in more suitable manner than he could for himself. But finally his own desires grew stronger. Faith reached out, timidly, tremblingly, yet it was real faith, and his soul was strengthened, until at last as Honorius ended, his tongue was loosed and uttered the cry of his heart—"Lord, I believe! Oh, help thou my unbelief!" The "one mediator between God and men, the man Christ Jesus," had become real to his faith; and the words of Jesus, "Verily, verily, I say unto you, He that heareth my word, and believeth on him that sent me, *hath* everlasting life, and shall not come into condemnation [judgment]; but is passed from death unto life. . . . And I *give* unto them [my sheep] eternal life; and they shall never perish, neither shall any man pluck them out of my hand," were received, believed, and rejoiced in.

Hours passed on. But who can fittingly describe the progress of a soul, passing from death unto life? Enough, that when morning dawned on the earth above, a glorious day had dawned on the soul and spirit of Marcellus in the vaults below. His longings were completely satisfied; the burden of sins was removed, and the peace of God, through Jesus Christ, filled him.

The Christian's secret was his and he had become the willing bondslave of Jesus Christ. One with his brethren in Christ he could now sing with them:

> Unto Him that loved us,
> To Him that washed us from our sins
> In His own blood,
> To Him be glory and dominion
> Forever and ever.

CHAPTER VI

THE CLOUD OF WITNESSES

These all died in faith.

T HE NEW CONVERT soon learned more of the Christians. After a brief repose he rose and was joined by Honorius, who offered to show him the nature of the place and where they lived.

Those whom he had seen at the chapel service formed but a small part of the dwellers in the Catacombs. Their numbers rose to many thousands, and they were scattered throughout its wide extent in little communities, each of which had its own means of communication with the city.

He walked far on, accompanied by Honorius. He was astonished at the numbers of people whom he encountered; and though he knew that the Christians were numerous, yet he did not suppose that so vast a proportion would have the fortitude to choose a life in the Catacombs.

Nor was he less interested in the dead than in the living. As he passed along he read the inscriptions upon their tombs, and found in them all the same strong faith and lofty hope. These he loved to read, and the fond interest which Honorius took in these pious memorials made him a congenial guide.

"There," said Honorius, "lies a witness for the truth."

Marcellus looked where he pointed, and read as follows:

PRIMITIUS, IN PEACE, AFTER MANY TOR-MENTS, A MOST VALIANT MARTYR. HE LIVED ABOUT THIRTY-EIGHT YEARS. HIS WIFE RAISED THIS TO HER DEAREST HUSBAND, THE WELL-DESERVING.

"These men," said Honorius, "show us how Christians ought to die. Yonder is another who suffered like Primitius."

PAULUS WAS PUT TO DEATH IN TORTURES, IN ORDER THAT HE MIGHT LIVE IN ETERNAL BLISS.

"And there," said Honorius, "is the tomb of a noble lady, who showed that fortitude which Christ can always bestow even to the weakest of His followers in the hour of need."

CLEMENTIA, TORTURED, DEAD, SLEEPS, WILL RISE.

"If called upon," said Honorius, "to pass through the article of death, the spirit is instantly 'absent from the body and present with the Lord.' The promised return of our Lord, which may be at any moment, is the 'blessed hope' of the instructed Christian. 'For the Lord himself shall descend from heaven with a shout, with the voice of the archangel, and with the trump of God: and the dead in Christ shall rise first: then we which are alive and remain shall be caught up together with them in the clouds, to meet the Lord in the air: and so shall we ever be with the Lord.' "

"Here," continued Honorius, "lies Constans, doubly constant to his God by a double trial. Poison was given to him first, but it was powerless over him, so he was put to the sword."

THE DEADLY DRAUGHT DARED NOT PRESENT TO CONSTANS THE CROWN WHICH THE STEEL WAS PERMITTED TO OFFER.

Thus they walked along reading the inscriptions which appeared on every side. New feelings came to Marcellus as he read the glorious catalogue of names. It was to him a history of the Church of Christ. Here were the acts of the martyrs portrayed before him in words that burned. The rude pictures that adorned many of the tombs carried with them a pathos that the finest works of the skillful artist could not produce. The rudely carved letters, the bad spelling and grammatical errors that characterized many of them, gave a touching proof of the treasure of the Gospel to the poor and lowly. "Not many wise, not many mighty are called"; but "to the poor the gospel is preached."

On many of them there was a monogram, which was formed of the initial letters of the titles of Christ (Χριστος Ραββουί, Christ the Lord), "X" and "P" being joined so as to form

one cipher. Some bore a palm branch, the emblem of victory and immortality, the token of that palm of glory which shall hereafter wave in the hands of the innumerable throng that are to stand around the throne. Others bore other devices.

"What is this?" said Marcellus, pointing to a picture of a ship.

"It shows that the redeemed spirit has sailed from earth to the haven of rest."

"And what is the meaning of this fish that I see represented so often?"

"The fish is used because the letters that form its name in Greek are the initials of words that express the glory and hope of the Christian. 'I' stands for 'Jesus,' 'X' for 'Christ,' 'Θ' and 'Υ' for 'the Son of God,' and 'Σ' for 'Saviour,' so that the fish symbolizes under its name 'ΙΧΘΥΣ' 'Jesus Christ, the Son of God, the Saviour.'"

"What means this picture that I see so often —a ship and a huge sea monster?"

"That is Jonah, a prophet of God, of whom as yet you are ignorant."

Honorius then related the account of Jonah, and showed him how the escape from the bowels of the fish reminded the Christian of his deliverance from the darkness of the tomb. "This glorious hope of the resurrection is an unspeakable comfort," said he, "and we love to bring it to our thoughts by different symbols. There, too, is another symbol of the same blessed truth—the dove carrying an olive branch to Noah." He related to his companion the account of the flood, so that Marcellus might see the meaning of the representation. "But of all the symbols which are used," said he, "none is so clear as this," and he pointed to a picture of the resurrection of Lazarus.

"There, too," said Honorius, "is an anchor, the sign of hope, by which the Christian, while tossing amid the stormy billows of life, holds on to his heavenly home.

"There you see the cock, the symbol for watchfulness; for our Lord has said, 'Watch and pray.' There also is the lamb, the type of innocence and gentleness, which also brings to our mind the Lamb of God, who bore our sins, and by whose sacrifice we receive eternal life and forgiveness. There again is the dove, which, like the lamb, represents innocence; and yet again you see it bearing the olive branch of peace.

"There are the letters Alpha and Omega, the first and last of the Greek alphabet, which represent our Lord; for you now know that He said, 'I am Alpha and Omega.' And there is the crown, which reminds of that incorruptible crown which the Lord, the righteous Judge, shall give us. Thus we love to surround ourselves with all that can remind us of the joy that lies before us. Taught by these, we look up from the surrounding gloom and by faith see above us the light of eternal glory."

"Here," said Marcellus, pausing, "is something that seems adapted to my condition. It sounds prophetic. Perhaps I too may be called upon to give my testimony for Christ. May I then be found faithful!"

IN CHRIST, IN THE TIME OF THE EMPEROR ADRIAN, MARIUS, A YOUNG MILITARY OFFICER, WHO LIVED LONG ENOUGH, AS HE SHED HIS BLOOD FOR CHRIST, AND DIED IN PEACE. HIS FRIENDS SET UP THIS WITH TEARS AND IN FEAR.

" 'In this world ye shall have tribulation; but be of good cheer, I have overcome the world.' Thus Christ assures us; but while He warns us of evil, He consoles us with His promise of support. In Him we can find grace sufficient for us."

"May the example of this young officer be for me," said Marcellus. "I may shed my blood for Christ like him. May I die as faithfully! To lie here among my brethren with such an epitaph, would be higher honor for me than a mausoleum like that of Cæcilia Metella."

They walked on as before.

"How sweet," said Marcellus, "is the death of the Christian! Its horror has fled. To him it is a blessed sleep, while the spirit is with the Lord awaiting the resurrection, and death, instead of awakening terror, is associated with thoughts of victory and of rest."

THE SLEEPING PLACE OF ELPIS

ZOTICUS LAID HERE TO SLEEP

ASELUS SLEEPS IN CHRIST

MARTYRIA IN PEACE

VIDALIA IN THE PEACE OF CHRIST

NICEPHORUS, A SWEET SOUL, IN THE PLACE OF
REFRESHMENT

"Some of those inscriptions tell of the characters of the departed brethren," said Honorius. "Look at these."

MAXIMIUS, WHO LIVED TWENTY-THREE YEARS,
FRIEND OF ALL MEN

IN CHRIST, ON THE FIFTH KALENDS OF
NOVEMBER, SLEPT GORGONIUS, FRIEND
OF ALL, AND ENEMY TO NONE.

"And here too," he continued, "are others which tell of their private lives and domestic experiences."

CAECILIUS THE HUSBAND, TO CAECILIA PLA-
CINDA, MY WIFE, OF EXCELLENT MEMORY,
WITH WHOM I LIVED TEN YEARS WITHOUT
ANY QUARREL, IN JESUS CHRIST, SON OF GOD,
THE SAVIOUR.

SACRED TO CHRIST THE SUPREME GOD. VITALIS,
BURIED ON SATURDAY, KALENDS OF AUGUST,
AGED TWENTY-FIVE YEARS AND EIGHT
MONTHS. SHE LIVED WITH HER HUSBAND
TEN YEARS AND THIRTY DAYS. IN CHRIST THE
FIRST AND THE LAST.

TO DOMNINA, MY SWEETEST AND MOST INNO-
CENT WIFE, WHO LIVED SIXTEEN YEARS AND
FOUR MONTHS, AND WAS MARRIED TWO
YEARS FOUR MONTHS AND NINE DAYS: WITH
WHOM I WAS NOT ABLE TO LIVE, ON ACCOUNT
OF MY TRAVELING, MORE THAN SIX MONTHS,
DURING WHICH TIME I SHEWED HER MY LOVE
AS I FELT IT. NONE ELSE SO LOVED EACH
OTHER. BURIED ON THE FIFTEENTH BEFORE
THE KALENDS OF JUNE.

TO CLAUDIUS, THE WELL-DESERVING AND AFFEC-
TIONATE, WHO LOVED ME. HE LIVED ABOUT
TWENTY-FIVE YEARS IN CHRIST.

"There is the tribute of a loving father," said
Marcellus, as he read the following:

LAURENCE TO HIS SWEETEST SON SEVERUS.
BORNE AWAY BY ANGELS ON THE
SEVENTH IDES OF JANUARY.

"And here of a wife."

Domitius in peace, Lea erected this.

"Yes," said Honorius, "by the faith of Jesus
Christ (or, as you would say, 'the religion') the
believer receives a new and divine nature, im-
parted by the Holy Spirit, who also implants in
him the love of God, which makes him suscepti-
ble to more tender affection to friends and relatives. The old Adam nature remains, however,
but is never improved, *nor can be.*"

Passing on, they found many epitaphs which
exhibited this tender love of departed relatives.

CONSTANTIA, OF WONDERFUL BEAUTY AND
AMIABILITY, WHO LIVED EIGHTEEN YEARS
SIX MONTHS AND SIXTEEN DAYS. CONSTANTIA
IN PEACE.

SIMPLICIUS, OF GOOD AND HAPPY MEMORY,
WHO LIVED TWENTY-THREE YEARS AND
FORTY-THREE DAYS IN PEACE. HIS
BROTHER MADE THIS MONUMENT.

TO ADSERTOR OUR SON, DEAR, SWEET, MOST IN-
NOCENT, AND INCOMPARABLE, WHO LIVED
SEVENTEEN YEARS SIX MONTHS AND EIGHT
DAYS. HIS FATHER AND MOTHER SET UP THIS.

TO JANUARIUS, SWEET AND GOOD SON, HONORED
AND BELOVED BY ALL: WHO LIVED TWENTY-
THREE YEARS FIVE MONTHS AND TWENTY-
TWO DAYS.

HIS PARENTS. LAURINIA, SWEETER THAN
HONEY, SLEEPS IN PEACE.

TO THE HOLY SOUL, INNOCENS, WHO LIVED
ABOUT THREE YEARS.

DOMITIANUS, AN INNOCENT SOUL, SLEEPS
IN PEACE.

*Farewell, O Sabina: she lived 8 years, 8 months and
22 days. Mayst thou live sweet in God.*

IN CHRIST: DIED ON THE KALENDS OF SEPTEM-
BER, POMPEIANUS THE INNOCENT, WHO
LIVED SIX YEARS, NINE MONTHS, EIGHT DAYS
AND FOUR HOURS. HE SLEEPS IN PEACE.

TO THEIR DESERVING SON, CALPURNIUS, HIS
PARENTS MADE THIS: HE LIVED FIVE YEARS,
EIGHT MONTHS AND TEN DAYS, AND DE-
PARTED IN PEACE ON THE THIRTEENTH OF
JUNE.

"Unto the epitaph of this child," said Marcellus, "they have added the symbols of peace
and of glory." He pointed to a child's tomb,
upon the slab of which was engraved a dove and
a laurel crown, together with the following inscription:

RESPECTUS, WHO LIVED FIVE YEARS AND EIGHT
MONTHS, SLEEPS IN PEACE.

"And this one," continued Marcellus, "has a
palm branch, the symbol of victory."

"Yes," said Honorius, "the Saviour has said,
'Suffer the little children to come unto me.'"

Their attention was also attracted by epitaphs
over the graves of women who had been wives
of Christian ministers.

MY WIFE LAURENTIA MADE ME THIS TOMB. SHE
WAS EVER SUITED TO MY DISPOSITION, VENER-
ABLE AND FAITHFUL. AT LENGTH DISAP-
POINTED ENVY LIES CRUSHED. THE BISHOP
LEO SURVIVED HIS EIGHTIETH YEAR.

THE PLACE OF BASIL THE PRESBYTER AND HIS
FELICITAS. THEY MADE IT FOR THEMSELVES.

ONCE THE HAPPY DAUGHTER OF THE PRESBY-
TER GABINUS, HERE LIES SUSANNA, JOINED
WITH HER FATHER IN PEACE.

CLAUDIUS ATTICIANUS, A LECTOR, AND
CLAUDIA FELICISSIMA HIS WIFE.

"I see here," said Marcellus, "a larger tomb. Are two buried here?"

"Yes, this is a 'bisomum,' and two occupy that cell. Read the inscription":

THE BISOMUM OF SABINUS. HE MADE IT FOR HIMSELF DURING HIS LIFETIME IN THE CEMETERY OF BALBINA IN THE NEW CRYPT.

"Sometimes," continued Honorius, "three are buried in the same grave. In other places, Marcellus, you will see that large numbers are buried; for when persecution rages, it is not always possible to pay to each individual the separate attention that is desired. Yonder is a tablet that marks the burial-place of many martyrs whose names are unknown, but whose memories are blessed." He pointed to a slab bearing the following inscription:

MARCELLA AND FIVE HUNDRED AND FIFTY MARTYRS OF CHRIST.

"Here is a longer one," said Marcellus, "and its words may well find an echo in the hearts of all of us." With deep emotion they read the following:

IN CHRIST. ALEXANDER IS NOT DEAD, BUT LIVES ABOVE THE STARS, AND HIS BODY RESTS IN THIS TOMB. HE ENDED HIS LIFE UNDER THE EMPEROR ANTONINE, WHO ALTHOUGH HE MIGHT HAVE FORESEEN THAT GREAT BENEFIT

WOULD RESULT FROM HIS SERVICES, REN-
DERED UNTO HIM HATRED INSTEAD OF FAVOR.
FOR WHILE ON HIS KNEES, AND ABOUT TO
SACRIFICE UNTO THE TRUE GOD, HE WAS LED
AWAY TO EXECUTION. O SAD TIMES! IN
WHICH EVEN AMONG SACRED RITES AND
PRAYERS, NOT EVEN IN CAVERNS COULD WE
BE SAFE. WHAT CAN BE MORE WRETCHED
THAN SUCH A LIFE? AND WHAT THAN SUCH
A DEATH? WHERE THEY CANNOT BE BURIED
BY THEIR FRIENDS AND RELATIONS! AT
LENGTH THEY SPARKLE IN HEAVEN. HE HAS
SCARCELY LIVED WHO HAS LIVED IN CHRIS-
TIAN TIMES.

"This," said Honorius, "is the resting place
of a well-loved brother, whose memory is still
cherished in all the churches. Around this tomb
we shall hold the agape[1] upon the anniversary
of his birthday. At this feast the barriers of different classes and ranks, of different kindreds
and tribes and tongues and peoples are all
broken down. We are all brethren in Christ
Jesus, for we remember that as Christ loved us,
so ought we also to love one another."

In this walk Marcellus had ample opportunity
to witness the presence of that fraternal love to
which Honorius alluded. He encountered men,
women, and children of every rank and of every
age. Men who had filled the highest stations in
Rome associated in friendly intercourse with
those who were scarcely above the level of
slaves; those who had once been cruel and re-

[1] Feast of love.

lentless persecutors, now associated in pleasant union with the former objects of their hate. The Jewish priest, released from the yoke of the Law which he could not keep, and which was "the ministry of death" to him, walked hand in hand with the once-hated Gentile. The Greek had beheld the foolishness of the Gospel transformed into infinite wisdom, and the contempt which he had once felt for the followers of Jesus had given place to tender affection. Selfishness and ambition, haughtiness and envy, all the baser passions of human life, seemed to have fled before the almighty power of Christian love. The faith of Christ dwelt in their hearts in all its fullness, and its blessed influences were seen here as they might not be witnessed elsewhere; not because its nature or its power had been changed for their sakes, but because the universal persecution which pressed on all alike had robbed them of earthly possessions, cut them off from worldly temptations and ambitions, and by the constraining love of Christ in the great sympathy of common suffering had drawn them closer to one another.

"The worship of the true God," said Honorius, "differs from all false worship. The heathen must enter into his temple, and there through the medium of the unholy priest offer over and over his sacrifice to demons, which can never take away sins. But for us Christ has offered Himself, without spot to God, the once-for-all sacrifice for sins forever. Every one of His followers can now approach God through

Christ, the blessed High Priest in the heavens, for each believer is made, through Jesus, a king and priest unto God. To us, then, it is a matter of no moment, as far as worship is concerned, whether our chapels are left unto us, or whether we are banished from them out of the sight of earth. Heaven is the throne of God and the universe is His temple, and each one of His children can lift up his voice from any place and at any time to worship the Father."

Marcellus' journey extended for a long time and for a great distance. Prepared as he was to find a great extent, he was still astonished at its vastness. The half had not been told him; and though he had traversed so much, he was told that this was but a fraction of the whole extent.

The average height of the passageways was about eight feet, but in many places it rose to twelve or fifteen feet. Then the frequent chapels and rooms which had been formed by widening the arches gave greater space to the inhabitants, and made it possible for them to live and move in greater freedom. Also, in some places there were narrow openings in the roof, through which faint rays of light passed from the upper air. These were chosen as places for resort, but not for living. The presence of the blessed light of day, however faint, was pleasant beyond expression, and served in some slight degree to mitigate the surrounding gloom.

Marcellus saw some places which had been

A PASSAGE IN THE CATACOMBS

walled up forming a sudden termination to the passageway, but other paths branched off and encircled them and went on as before. "What is this place which is thus enclosed?" he asked.

"It is a Roman tomb," said Honorius. "On excavating this passage the workmen struck upon it, so they stopped and walled up the place and carried on their excavation around it. It was not from the fear of disturbing the tomb, but because in death, no less than in life, the Christian desires to follow the command of his Lord, and 'come out from among them, and be ye separate.'"

"Persecution rages around us and shuts us in," said Marcellus. "How long shall the people of God be scattered, how long shall the enemy distress us?"

"Such are the cries of many among us," said Honorius, "but it is wrong to complain. The Lord has been good to His people. Throughout the empire they have gone on for generations protected by the laws and unmolested. True, we have had terrible persecutions, in which thousands have died in agony, but these again have passed away and left the Church in peace.

"All the persecutions which we have yet received have served only to purify the hearts of the people of God and exalt their faith. He knows what is best for us. We are in His hands, and He will give us no more than we can bear. Let us be sober and watch and pray, O Marcellus, for the present storm tells us plainly that 'the great and terrible day' so long prophesied for the world is drawing near."

Thus Marcellus walked about with Honorius, conversing and learning new things every hour about the doctrines of God's truth and the experiences of His people. The evidences of their love, their purity, their fortitude, their faith sank deeply into his soul.

The experience which he too had felt was not transient. Every new sight but strengthened his desire to unite himself with the faith and fortunes of the people of God. Accordingly, before the following Lord's Day, he was baptized "unto the death of Christ," in the name of the Father, and the Son, and the Holy Ghost.

On the morning of the Lord's Day he sat around the Table of the Lord in company with other Christians. There they held that simple and affecting feast of remembrance at the Lord's Table, by which the Christians showed forth the death of Jesus, while waiting for His return. Honorius offered up the prayer of thanksgiving for the repast. And for the first time Marcellus partook of the bread and the wine, the sacred symbols of the body and blood of his crucified Lord.

"And when they had sung a hymn, they went out."

CHAPTER VII

THE CONFESSION OF FAITH

*Yea, and all that will live godly in Christ Jesus
shall suffer persecution.*

FOUR DAYS HAD ELAPSED since the young soldier had left his chamber. Eventful days they
had been to him, days full of infinite importance.
Endless weal or woe had hung upon their issue.
But the search of this earnest soul after the truth
had not been in vain, "being born again of the
Holy Ghost."

His resolution had been taken. On the one
side lay fame, honor, and wealth; on the other,
poverty, want, and woe; yet he had made his
choice, and turned to the latter without a moment's hesitation. He chose "rather to suffer
affliction with the people of God, than to enjoy
the pleasures of sin for a season."

Upon his return he visited the general and
reported himself. He informed him that he had
been among the Christians, that he could not
execute his commission, and was willing to take
the consequences. The general sternly ordered
him to his quarters.

Here in the midst of deep meditation, while

conjecturing what might be the issue of all this, he was interrupted by the entrance of Lucullus. His friend greeted him most affectionately, but was evidently full of anxiety.

"I have just seen the general," said he, "who sent for me to give me a message for you. But first tell me what is this that you have done?"

Marcellus then related everything from the time he had left until his return, concealing nothing whatever. His deep earnestness showed how strong and true and eternal was the work of the Spirit in him. He then related his interview with his general.

"I entered the room feeling the importance of the step I was taking. I was about to commit an act of virtual treason, a crime which can only be punished with death. Yet I could do nothing else.

"He received me graciously, for he thought that I had met with some important success in my search. I told him that since I left I had been among the Christians, and from what I had seen of them I had been forced to change my feelings toward them. I had thought that they were enemies of the State and worthy of death, but I found that they were loyal subjects of the emperor and virtuous men. I could never use my sword against such as these, and rather than do so I would give it up.

" 'A soldier's feelings,' said he, 'have no right to interfere with his duties.'

" 'But my duties to the God who made me are stronger than any which I owe to man.'

" 'Has your sympathy with the Christians made you mad?' said he. 'Do you not know that this is treason?'

"I bowed, and said that I would take the consequences.

" 'Rash youth,' he cried sternly, 'go to your quarters, and I will communicate to you my decision.'

"And so I came here at once, and have been here ever since then, anxiously awaiting my sentence."

Lucullus had listened to the whole of Marcellus' recital without a word or even a gesture. An expression of sad surprise upon his face told what his feelings were. He spoke in a mournful tone as Marcellus ended.

"And what that sentence must be you certainly know as well as I. Roman discipline, even in ordinary times, can never be trifled with, but now the feelings of the government are excited to an unusual degree against these Christians. If you persist in your present course, you must fall."

"I have told you all my reasons."

"I know, Marcellus, your pure and sincere nature. You have always been of a devout mind. You have loved the noble teachings of philosophy. Can you not satisfy yourself with these as before? Why should you be attracted by the wretched doctrine of a crucified Jew?"

"I have never been satisfied with the philosophy of which you speak. You yourself know that there is nothing certain in it on which the soul may rest. But Christianity is the truth of God, brought down by Himself, and sanctified by His own death."

"You have thoroughly explained the whole Christian creed to me. Your own enthusiasm has made it appear attractive, I will confess; and if all its followers were really like yourself, my dear Marcellus, it might be adapted to bless the world. But I come not here to argue upon religion. I come to speak about yourself. You are in danger, my dear friend; your station, your honor, your office, your very life are at stake. Consider what you have done. An important commission was entrusted to you, upon the execution of which you set out. It was expected that you would return bringing important information. But instead of this you come back and inform the general that you have gone over to the enemy, that you are one of them in heart, and that you refuse to bear arms against them. If the soldier is free to choose whom he will fight, what becomes of discipline? He must obey orders. Am I right?"

"You are, Lucullus."

"The question for you to decide is not whether you will choose philosophy or Christianity, but whether you will be a Christian or a soldier. For as the times are now you see that it is impossible for you to be a soldier and a Christian at the same time. One of the two must be given up. And not only so, but if you decide upon being a Christian, you must at once share their fate, for no distinction can be made in favor of you. On the other hand, if you continue a soldier, you must fight against the Christians."

"That is no doubt the question."

"You have warm friends who are willing to forget your great offense, Marcellus. I know your enthusiastic nature, and I have pleaded with the general for you. He too respects you for your soldierly qualities. He is willing to forgive you under certain circumstances."

"What are they?"

"The most merciful of all conditions. Let the past four days be forgotten; banish them from your memory. Resume your commission. Take your soldiers and go at once about your duty in arresting these Christians."

"Lucullus," said Marcellus, rising from his seat with folded arms, "I love you as a friend, I am grateful for your faithful affection. Never can I forget it. But I have that within me now to which you are a stranger, which is stronger than all honors of State. It is the love of God. For this I am ready to give up all, honor, rank, and life itself. My decision is irrevocable. I am a Christian."

For a moment Lucullus sat in astonishment and grief looking at his friend. He was well acquainted with his resolute soul, and saw with pain how completely his persuasions had failed. At length he spoke again. He used every argument that he could think of. He brought forward every motive that might influence him. He told him of the terrible fate that awaited him, and the peculiar vengeance that would be directed against him; but all his words were completely useless. At length he rose in deep sadness.

"Marcellus," he said, "you tempt fate. You are rushing madly upon a terrible destiny. Everything that fortune can bestow is before you, but you turn away from all to cast your lot among wretched outcasts. I have done the duty of a friend in trying to turn you from your folly, but all that I can do is of no avail.

"I have brought you the sentence of the general. You are degraded from office. You are put under arrest as a Christian. Tomorrow you will be seized and handed over to punishment. But many hours are yet before you, and I may still have the mournful satisfaction of assisting you to escape. Fly then at once. Hasten, for there is no time to lose. There is only one place in the world where you can be secure from the vengeance of Cæsar."

Marcellus heard in silence. Slowly he took off his splendid arms and laid them down, sadly he unfastened his gorgeous armor which he had worn so proudly. He stood in his simple tunic before his friend.

"Lucullus, again I say that I can never forget your faithful friendship. Would we were flying together, that your prayers might ascend with mine to Him whom I serve. But enough; I will go. Farewell."

"Farewell, Marcellus. We may never meet in

life again. If you are ever in want or peril, you know on whom you can rely."

The two young men embraced, and Marcellus hastily took his departure.

He walked out of the camp and onward until he reached the Forum. All around him were stately marble temples and columns and monuments. There the arch of Titus spanned the *Via Sacra;* there the imperial palace reared its gigantic form on high, rich in stately architecture, in glorious adornments of precious marbles, and glowing in golden decorations. On one side the lofty walls of the Coliseum arose; beyond, the stupendous dome of the Temple of Peace; and on the other the Capitoline Hill upraised its historic summit, crowned with a cluster of stately temples that stood out in sharp relief against the sky.

To this he directed his steps, and ascended the steep declivity up to the top of the hill. From the summit he looked around upon the scene. The place itself was a spacious square paved with marble, and surrounded with lordly temples. On one side was the Campus Martius, bounded by the Tiber, whose yellow flood wound afar onward to the Mediterranean. On every other side the city spread its unequaled extent, crowding to the narrow walls, and overleaping them to throw out its radiating streets far away on every side into the country. Temples and columns and monuments reared their lofty heads. Innumerable statues filled the streets with a population of sculptured forms, fountains dashed into the air, chariots rolled through the streets, the legions of Rome marched to and fro in military array, and on every side surged the restless tide of life in the Imperial City.

Far away the plain extended, dotted with countless villages and houses and palaces, rich in luxuriant verdure, the dwelling place of peace and plenty. On one side arose the blue outline of the Apennines, crowned with snow; on the other the dark waves of the Mediterranean washed the far-distant shore.

Suddenly Marcellus was startled by a shout. He turned. An old man in scant clothing, with emaciated face and frenzied gesticulation, was shouting out a strain of fearful denunciation. His wild glance and fierce manner showed that he was partly insane.

Babylon the great is fallen, is fallen,
And is become the habitation of devils,
And the hold of every foul spirit,
And a cage of every unclean and hateful bird;

*   *   *

For God hath remembered her iniquities.
Reward her even as she rewarded you,
And double unto her double according to her
    works. . . .
How much she hath glorified herself, and lived
    deliciously. . . .
Therefore shall her plagues come in one day,
Death, and mourning, and famine;
And she shall be utterly burned with fire;

For strong is the Lord God who judgeth her.
The kings of the earth . . .
Shall bewail her, and lament for her . . .
Seeing the smoke of her burning,
Standing afar off for fear of her torment,
Saying, Alas, alas, that great city Babylon,
That mighty city!
For in one hour is thy judgment come.
The merchants of the earth . . .
Stand afar off for fear of her torment,
Weeping and wailing,
Saying, Alas, alas, that great city,
That was clothed in fine linen, and purple, and
    scarlet,
And decked with gold, and precious stones, and
    pearls!
For in one hour so great riches is come to naught.
And every shipmaster, and the company in ships,
And sailors and as many as trade by sea,
Shall cry when they see the smoke of her burning,
Stood afar off, and cried . . .
What city is like unto that great city!
And they cast dust on their heads and cried,
Weeping and wailing, saying,
Alas, alas, that great city,
Wherein were made rich all that had ships in the
    sea . . .
For in one hour is she made desolate.
Rejoice over her, thou heaven,
And ye holy apostles and prophets,
For God hath avenged you on her.

A vast crowd collected around him in amazement, but scarcely had he ceased when some
soldiers appeared and led him away.

"Doubtless it is some poor Christian whose brain has been turned by suffering," thought Marcellus. As the man was led away, he still shouted out his terrific denunciations, and a great crowd followed, yelling and deriding. Soon the noise died away in the distance.

"There is no time to lose. I must go," said Marcellus; and he turned away.

CHAPTER VIII

LIFE IN THE CATACOMBS

O dark, dark, dark, amid the blaze of noon,
Irrevocably dark, total eclipse,
Without all hope of day!

UPON HIS RETURN to the Catacombs he was welcomed with tears of joy. Most eagerly they listened to the account of his interview with his superiors; and while they sympathized with his troubles, they rejoiced that he had been found worthy to suffer for Christ.

Amid these new scenes he learned more of the truth every day, and saw what its followers endured. Life in the Catacombs opened around him with all its wondrous variety.

The vast numbers who dwelt below were supplied with provisions by constant communication with the city above. This was done at night. The most resolute and daring of the men volunteered for this dangerous task. Sometimes also women, and even boys, went forth upon this errand, and the lad Pollio was the most acute and successful of all these. Amid the vast population of Rome it was not difficult to pass unnoticed, and consequently the supply was well

kept up. Yet sometimes the journey met with a
fatal termination, and the bold adventurers
never returned.

Of water there was a plentiful supply in the
passageways of the lowermost tier. Wells and
fountains here supplied sufficient for all their
wants.

At night, too, were made the most mournful
expeditions of all. These were in search of the
dead which had been torn by the wild beasts or
burned at the stake. These loved remains were
obtained at the greatest risk, and brought down
amid a thousand dangers. Then the friends of
the lost would perform the funeral service and
hold the burial feast. After this they would de-
posit their remains in the narrow cell, and close
the place up with a marble tablet graven with
the name of the occupant.

The ancient Christian, inspired by the glorious doctrine of the resurrection, looked forward
with ardent hope to the time when corruption
should put on incorruption, and the mortal, immortality. He was unwilling that the body
which so sublime a destiny awaited should be re-
duced to ashes, and thought that even the sacred
funeral flames were a dishonor to that temple of
God which had been so highly favored of
Heaven. So the cherished bodies of the dead
were brought here out of the sight of man, where
no irreverent hand might disturb the solemn
stillness of their last repose, to lie until "the last
trump" should give that summons for which
the primitive Church waited so eagerly, in daily

expectation. In the city above, Christianity had been increasing for successive generations, and during all this time the dead had been coming here in ever-increasing numbers, so that now the Catacombs formed a vast city of the dead, whose silent population slumbered in endless ranges, rank above rank, waiting till the Lord's shout of assembly should call His blood-washed people, "in a moment, in the twinkling of an eye" to meet Him in the air.

In many places the arches had been knocked away and the roof heightened so as to form rooms. None of them were of very great size, but they formed areas where the fugitives might meet in larger companies and breathe more freely. Here they passed much of the time, and here, too, they held their assemblies of fellowship.

The nature of the times in which they lived will explain their situation. The simple virtues of the old republic had passed away, and freedom had taken her everlasting flight. Corruption had moved over the empire and subdued everything beneath its numbing influence. Plots, rebellions, treasons, and strikes cursed the State by turns, but the fallen people stood by in silence. They saw their bravest suffer, their noblest die, all unmoved. The generous heart, the soul of fire, wakened no more. Only the basest passions aroused their degenerate feelings.

Into such a state as this the truth of Christ came boldly, and through such enemies as these it had to fight its way over such obstacles to make its slow but sure progress. They who enlisted under her banner had no life of ease before them. Her trumpet gave forth no uncertain sound. The conflict was stern, and involved name, and fame, and fortune, and friends, and life—all that was most dear to man. Time rolled on. If the followers of truth increased in number, so also did vice intensify her power and her malignity; the people sank into deeper corruption, the State drifted on to more certain ruin.

Then arose those terrible persecutions which aimed to obliterate from the earth the last vestiges of Christianity. A terrible ordeal awaited the Christian if he resisted the imperial decree; to those who followed her, the order of Truth was inexorable; and when a decision was made, it was a final one. To make that decision for Christianity was often to accept instant death, or else to be driven from the city, banished from the joys of home and from the light of day.

The hearts of the Romans were hardened and their eyes blinded. Neither childhood's innocence, nor womanly purity, nor noble manhood, nor the reverend hairs of age, nor faith immovable, nor love triumphant over death, could touch them or move them to pity. They did not see the black cloud of desolation that hovered over the doomed empire, or know that from its fury those whom they persecuted alone could save them.

Yet in that reign of terror the Catacombs opened before the Christians like a city of refuge. Here lay the bones of their fathers who

from generation to generation had fought for
the truth, and their worn bodies waited here for
the resurrection shout. Here they brought their
relatives. as one by one they had left them and
gone on high. Here the son had borne the body
of his aged mother, and the parent had seen his
child committed to the tomb. Here they had
carried the mangled remains of those who had
been torn to pieces by wild beasts in the arena,
the blackened corpses of those who had been
given to the flames, or the wasted bodies of those
most wretched who had sighed out their lives
amid the lingering agonies of death by crucifixion. Every Christian had some friend or rela-
tive lying here in death. The very ground was
sanctified, the very air hallowed. It was not
strange that they should seek safety in such a
place.

Moreover, in these subterranean abodes they
found their only place of refuge from persecution. They could not seek foreign countries or
flee beyond the sea because for them there were
no countries of refuge, and no lands beyond the
sea held out a hope. The imperial power of
Rome grasped the civilized world in its mighty
embrace; her tremendous police system extended through all lands, and none might escape
her wrath. So resistless was this power, that
from the highest noble down to the meanest
slave—all were subject to it. The dethroned
emperor could not escape her vengeance, or was
such an escape even hoped for. When Nero
fell, he could only go and kill himself in a neigh-

boring villa. Yet here, amid these infinite labyrinths, even the power of Rome was unavailing,
and her baffled emissaries faltered at the very
entrance.

Here, then, the persecuted Christians tarried,
and their great numbers peopled these paths and
grottoes; by day assembling to exchange words
of cheer and comfort, or to bewail the death of
some new martyr; by night sending forth the
boldest among them, like a forlorn hope, to learn
tidings of the upper world, or to bring down
the blood-stained bodies of some new victims.
Through the different persecutions, they lived
here so secure that although millions perished
throughout the empire, the power of Christianity at Rome was but slightly shaken.

Their safety was secured and life preserved,
but on what terms? For what is life without
light, or what is the safety of the body in gloom
that depresses the soul? The physical nature of
man shrinks from such a fate, and his delicate
organization is speedily aware of the lack of that
subtle renovating principle which is connected
with light only. One by one the functions of the
body lose their tone and energy. This weakening
of the body affects the mind, predisposing it to
gloom, apprehension, doubt, and despair. It is
greater honor for a man to be true and steadfast
under such circumstances than to have died a
heroic death in the arena or to have perished
unflinchingly at the stake. Here, where there
closed around these captives the thickest shades
of darkness, they encountered their sorest trial.

Fortitude under the persecution itself was admirable; but against the persecution, blended with such horrors as these, it became sublime.

The cold blast that forever drifted through these labyrinths chilled them, but brought no pure air from above; the floors, the walls, the roofs were covered over with the foul deposits of damp vapors that forever hung around; the atmosphere was thick with impure exhalations and poisonous miasma; the dense smoke from the ever-burning torches might have mitigated the noxious gases, but it oppressed the dwellers here with its blinding and suffocating influence. Yet amid all these accumulated horrors the soul of the martyr stood up unconquered. The quickened spirit that endured all this rose up to grander proportions than were ever attained in the proudest days of the old republic. The fortitude of Regulus, the devotion of Curtius, the constancy of Brutus, were here surpassed, not only by the strong man, but by the tender virgin and the weak child. Thus, scorning to yield to the fiercest power of persecution, these men went forth, the good, the pure in heart, the brave, the noble. For them death had no terrors, or that appalling life in death which they were compelled to endure here in the dismal regions of the dead. They knew what was before them, and they accepted it all. Willingly they descended here, carrying with them all that was most precious to the soul of man, and they endured all for the great love wherewith they were loved.

The constant efforts which they made to diminish the gloom of their abodes were visible all around. The walls were in some places covered over with white stucco, and in others these again were adorned with pictures, not of deified mortals for idolatrous worship, but of those grand old heroes of the truth who had "through faith subdued kingdoms, wrought righteousness, obtained promises, stopped the mouths of lions, quenched the violence of fire, escaped the edge of the sword, out of weakness were made strong, waxed valiant in fight, turned to flight the armies of the aliens" (Heb. 11:33, 34). If in the hour of bitter anguish they sought for scenes or thoughts that might relieve their souls and inspire them with fresh strength for the future, they could have found no other objects to look upon, so strong to encourage, so mighty to console.

Such were the decorations of the chapels. The only furniture which they contained was a simple wooden table upon which they placed the bread and wine of the Lord's Supper, the symbols of the body and blood of their crucified Lord.

Christianity had struggled long, and it was a struggle with corruption. It will not be thought strange, then, if the Church contracted some *marks* of a too close contact with her foe, or if she carried some of them down to her place of refuge. Yet if they had some variations from the apostolic model, these were so trifling that they might be overlooked altogether, were it not that they opened the way to greater ones. Still, the essential doctrines of Christianity knew no pollution, no change. The guilt of man, the mercy of the Father, the atonement of the Son, the indwelling of the Holy Spirit, salvation through faith in the Redeemer, the value of His precious blood, His physical resurrection, the blessed hope of His return—all these foundation truths were cherished with a fervor and an energy to which no language can do justice.

Theirs was that heavenly hope, the anchor of the soul, so strong and so secure that the storm of an empire's wrath failed to drive them from the Rock of Ages where they were sheltered.

Theirs was that lofty faith which upheld them through the sorest trials. The glorified Man at God's right hand was the Object of their faith and hope. Faith in Him was everything. It was the very breath of life; so true that it upheld them in the hour of cruel sacrifices; so lasting that even when it seemed that all the followers of Christ had vanished from the earth, they could still look up trustfully and wait for Him.

Theirs was that love which Christ when on earth defined as comprising all the law and the prophets. Sectarian strife, denominational bitterness were unknown. They had a great general foe to fight; how could they quarrel with one another? Here arose love to man which knew no distinction of race or class, but embraced all in its immense circumference, so that one could lay down his life for his brother; here the love of God, shed abroad in the heart by

the Holy Spirit, stopped not at the sacrifice of
life itself. The persecutions which raged around
them strengthened in them all that zeal, faith,
and love which glowed so brightly amid the
darkness of the age. It confined their numbers to
the true and the sincere. It was the antidote to
hypocrisy. It gave to the brave the most daring
heroism, and inspired the fainthearted with the
courage of devotion. *They lived in a time when
to be a Christian was to risk one's life.* They
did not shrink, but boldly proclaimed their faith
and accepted the consequences. They drew a
broad line between themselves and the world,
and stood manfully on their own side. To utter
a few words, to perform a simple act, could often
save from death; but the tongue refused to speak
the idolatrous formula, and the stubborn hand
refused to pour the libation. The vital doctrines
of Christianity met from them far more than a
mere intellectual response. Christ Himself was
not to them an idea, a thought, but a real per-
sonal existence. The life of Jesus upon earth was
to them a living truth. They accepted it as a
proper example for every man. His gentleness,
humility, patience, and meekness they believed
were offered for imitation; nor did they ever
separate the ideal Christian from the real. They
thought that a man's faith consisted as much in
the life as in the sentiment, and had not learned
to separate experimental from practical Christianity. To them the death of Christ was a great
event to which all others were but secondary.
That He died in very deed, and for the sons of

men, none could understand better than they. That He is risen and glorified at God's right hand, all power given to Him in Heaven and on earth, was to them divine reality. Among their own brethren they could think of many a one who had hung upon the cross for his brethren or died at the stake for his God. They took up the cross and followed Christ, bearing His reproach. That cross and that reproach were not figurative. Witness these gloomy labyrinths, fit home for the dead only, which nevertheless for years opened to shelter the living. Witness these names of martyrs, those words of triumph. The walls carry down to later ages the words of grief, of lamentation, and of ever-changing feeling which were marked upon them during successive ages by those who were banished to these Catacombs. They carry down their mournful story to future times, and bring to imagination the forms, the feelings, and the deeds of those who were imprisoned here. As the forms of life are taken upon the plates of the camera, so has the great voice once forced out by suffering from the very soul of the martyr become stamped upon the wall.

Humble witnesses of the truth, poor, despised, forsaken, in vain their calls for mercy went forth to the ears of man; they were stifled in the blood of the slaughtered and the smoke of the sacrifice! Yet where their own race only answered their cry of despair with fresh tortures these rocky walls proved more merciful; they heard their sighs, they took them to their bosoms, and so their cries of suffering lived here, treasured up and graven in the rock forever.

The conversion of Marcellus to Christianity had been sudden. Yet such quick transitions from error to truth were not infrequent. He had tried the highest forms of pagan superstition and heathen philosophy but had found them wanting, and as soon as Christianity appeared before him, he beheld all that he desired. It possessed exactly what was needed to satisfy the cravings of his soul and fill his empty heart with the fullness of peace. And if the transition was quick, it was nonetheless thorough. Having opened his eyes and seen the light of the Sun of Righteousness, he could not close them. The work of regeneration was divinely thorough and he gladly welcomed his share in the sufferings of the persecuted.

Conversions like these distinguished the first preaching of the Gospel. Throughout the heathen world there were countless souls who felt as Marcellus did, and had gone through the same experiences. It needed only the preaching of the truth, accompanied by the power of the Holy Spirit, to open their eyes and bring them to see the light. Combined with divine influence over human reason, we see here a cause for the rapid spread of Christianity.

Living and moving and conversing with his new brethren, Marcellus soon began to enter into all their hopes and fears and joys. Their faith and trust communicated themselves to his heart, and all the glorious expectations which sustained them became the solace of his own soul. The blessed Word of life became his constant study and delight, and all its teachings found in him an ardent disciple.

Meetings for prayer and praise were frequent throughout the Catacombs. Cut off from ordinary occupations of worldly business, they were thrown entirely upon other and higher pursuits. Deprived of the opportunity to make efforts for the support of the body, they were constrained to make their chief business the care of the soul. They gained what they sought. Earth with its cares, its allurements, and its thousand attractions lost its hold upon them. Heaven drew nearer; their thoughts and their language were of the kingdom. They loved to talk of the joy that awaited those who continued faithful unto death; to converse upon those departed brethren who to them were not lost but gone before; to anticipate the moment when their own time should come. Above all, they looked every day for that great final summons which should raise the dead, transform the living, and bring His blood-bought, blood-washed people about Him in the meeting place in the air; and for the judgment seat of Christ, where He will bestow the rewards for faithful service (I Thess. 4:13-18; Phil. 3:20, 21; I Cor. 3).

Thus Marcellus saw these dismal passages not left to the silent slumber of the dead, but filled with thousands of the living. Wan and pale and oppressed, they found even amid this darkness a better fate than that which might await them above. Busy life animated the haunts of the dead; the pathways rang to the sound of human voices. The light of truth and virtue, banished from the upper air, burned anew with a purer radiance amid this subterranean gloom. The tender greetings of affection, of friendship, of kinship, and of love, arose amid the moldering remains of the departed. Here the tear of grief mingled with the blood of the martyr, and the hand of affection wrapped his pale limbs in the shroud. Here in these grottoes the heroic soul rose up superior to sorrow. Hope and faith smiled exultingly, and pointed to the light of "the bright and morning star," and the voice of praise breathed forth from the lips of the mourner.

CHAPTER IX

THE PERSECUTION

*Ye have need of patience, that after ye have done
the will of God ye might receive the promise.*

THE PERSECUTION RAGED with greater fury.
In the few weeks that passed since Marcellus
had lived here, great numbers had sought refuge
in this retreat. Never before had so many congregated here. Generally, the authorities had
been content with the more conspicuous Christians, and the fugitives to the Catacombs were
consequently composed of this class; it was a
severe persecution indeed which embraced all,
and such indiscriminate rage had been shown
only under a few emperors. But now there was
no distinction of class or station. The humblest
follower as well as the highest teacher was hurried away to death.

Until this time the communication with the
city was comparatively easy, for the poor Christians above ground never neglected those below
or forgot their wants. Provisions and assistance
of all kinds were readily obtained. But now the
very ones on whom the fugitives relied for help
were themselves driven out, to share their fate

and become the partakers, instead of the bestowers, of charity.

Still their situation was not desperate. There were many left in Rome who loved them and assisted them, although they were not Christians. In every great movement there will be an immense class composed of neutrals, who either from interest or indifference remain unmoved. These people will invariably join the strongest side, and where danger threatens will evade it by any concessions. Such was the condition of large numbers in Rome. They had friends and relatives among the Christians whom they loved, and for whom they felt sympathy. They were always ready to assist them, but had too much regard for their own safety to cast in their own lot with them. They attended the temples and assisted at the worship of the heathen gods as before, and were nominally adherents of the old superstition. Upon these now the Christians were forced to depend for the necessities of life.

The expeditions to the city were now accompanied with greater danger, and only the boldest dared to venture. Such, however, was the contempt of danger and death with which they were inspired that there was never any scarcity of men for this perilous duty.

To this task Marcellus offered himself, glad that he could in any way do good to his brethren. His fearlessness and acuteness, which had formerly raised him so high as a soldier, now made him conspicuous for success in this new pursuit.

THE COLISEUM

Numbers were destroyed every day. Their bodies were sought for and carried away by the Christians for purposes of burial. This was not very difficult to accomplish, since it relieved the authorities of the trouble of burning or burying the corpses.

One day tidings came to the community beneath the Appian Way that two of their number had been captured and put to death. Marcellus and another Christian went forth to obtain their bodies. The boy Pollio also went with them, to be useful in case of need. It was dusk when they entered the city gate, and darkness came rapidly on. Soon, however, the moon arose and illumined the scene.

They threaded their way through the dark streets, and at length came to the Coliseum, the place of martyrdom for so many of their companions. Its dark form towered up grandly before them, vast and gloomy and stern as the imperial power that reared it. Crowds of keepers and guards and gladiators were within the iron gates, where the vaulted passageways were illuminated with the glare of torches.

The keepers knew their errand, and rudely ordered them to follow. They led them on till they came to the arena. Here lay a number of bodies, the last of those who had been slain that day. They were fearfully mangled; some indeed were scarcely distinguishable as human beings. After a long search they found the two whom they sought. Their bodies were then placed in large sacks, in which they prepared to carry them away.

Marcellus looked in upon the scene. All around him rose the massive walls, ascending by many terraces back to the outer circle. Its black form seemed to shut him in with a barrier which he could not pass.

"How long will it be," he thought, "before I too shall take my place here and lay down my life for my Saviour? When that time comes shall I be true? Lord Jesus, in that hour sustain me!"

The moon had not yet risen high enough to shine into the arena. Within it was dark and forbidding. The search had been made with torches obtained from the keepers.

At this moment Marcellus heard a deep voice from some of the vaults behind them. Its tones rang out upon the night air with startling distinctness, and were heard high above the rude clamor of the keepers:

Now is come salvation, and strength,
And the kingdom of our God,
And the power of his Christ:
For the accuser of our brethren is cast down,
Which accused them before our God day and
    night.
And they overcame him by the blood of the
    Lamb,
And by the word of their testimony,
And they loved not their lives unto the death.

"Who is that?" said Marcellus.

"Do not notice him," said his companion. "It

is Brother Cinna. His griefs have made him mad. His only son was burned at the stake at the beginning of the persecution, and since then he has gone about the city denouncing woe. Hitherto they have let him alone; but now at last they have seized him."

"And is he a prisoner here?"

"He is."

Again the voice of Cinna arose, fearfully, menacingly, and terribly:

> How long, O Lord, holy and true,
> Dost thou not avenge our blood on
> Them that dwell upon the earth?

"This, then, is the man that I heard in the Capitol?"

"Yes. He has been all through the city, and even in the palace, uttering his cry."

"Let us go."

They took their sacks and started for the gates. After a short delay they were allowed to pass. As they went out they heard the voice of Cinna in the distance:

> Babylon the great is fallen, is fallen,
> And is become the habitation of devils,
> And the hold of every foul spirit,
> And the cage of every unclean and hateful bird:

*   *   *

> Come out of her, my people.

None of them spoke until they had reached a safe distance from the Coliseum.

"I felt afraid," said Marcellus, "that we should be kept in there."

"Your fears were reasonable," said the other. "Any sudden whim of the keeper might be our doom. But this we must be prepared for. In times like this we must be ready to meet death at any moment. What says our Lord? 'Be ye also ready.' We must be able to say when the time comes, 'I am now ready to be offered.'"

"Yes," said Marcellus, "our Lord has told us what we will have: 'In the world ye shall have tribulation—'

"And He says also, 'Be of good cheer; I have overcome the world. . . . Where I am, there ye shall be also.'"

"Through Him," said Marcellus, "we can come off more than conquerors over death. The afflictions of this present time are not worthy to be compared to the glory that shall be revealed to us."

Thus they solaced themselves with the promises of that blessed Word of life which in all ages and under all circumstances can give such heavenly consolation. Bearing their burdens, they finally reached their destination in safety, thankful that they had been preserved.

A few days afterward Marcellus went up for provisions. This time he was alone. He went to the house of a man who was friendly to them and had been of much assistance. It was outside of the walls, in the suburb nearest the Appian Way

After obtaining the requisite supply, he began to inquire after the news.

"The news is bad for you," said the man. "One of the Prætorian officers was recently converted to Christianity, and the emperor is enraged. He has appointed another to the office which he held, and has sent him after the Christians. They are catching some every day. No man is too poor to be seized in these days."

"Ah! Do you know the name of this Prætorian officer who is seeking the Christians?"

"Lucullus."

"Lucullus!" cried Marcellus. "How strange!"

"He is said to be a man of great skill and energy."

"I have heard of him. This is indeed bad news for the Christians."

"The conversion of the other Prætorian officer has greatly enraged the emperor. A price is now set upon his head. If you chance to see him or be in his way, friend, you had better let him know. They say he is in the Catacombs."

"He must be there. There is no other place of safety."

"These are indeed terrible times. You have need to be cautious."

"They cannot kill me more than once," said Marcellus.

"Ah, you Christians have wonderful fortitude. I admire your bravery; yet I think you might conform outwardly to the emperor's decree. Why should you rush so madly upon death?"

"Our Redeemer died for us. We are ready to die for Him. And since He died for His people, we also are willing to imitate Him and lay down our lives for our brethren."

"You are wonderful people," said the man, raising his hands.

Marcellus now bade him farewell, and departed with his load. The news which he had just heard filled his mind.

"So Lucullus has taken my place," thought he. "I wonder if he has turned against me. Does he now think of me as his friend Marcellus, or only as a Christian? I may soon find out. It would be strange indeed if I should fall into his hands; and yet if I am captured, it will probably be by him.

"Yet it is his duty as a soldier, and why should I complain? If he is appointed to that office, he can do nothing else than obey. As a soldier he can only treat me as an enemy of the State. He may pity or love me in his heart, yet he must not shrink from his duty.

"If a price is put on my head they will redouble their efforts for me. My time, I believe, is at hand. Let me be prepared to meet it."

With such thoughts as these he walked down the Appian Way. He was wrapped up in his own meditations, and did not see a crowd of people that had gathered at a corner of a street until he was among them. Then he suddenly found himself stopped.

"Ho, friend," cried a rude voice, "not so fast! Who are you, and where are you going?"

"Away," cried Marcellus in a tone of command natural to one who had ruled over men; and he motioned the man aside.

The crowd was awe-struck by his authoritative tone and imperious manner, but its spokesman showed more courage.

"Tell us who you are, or you shall not pass."

"Fellow," cried Marcellus, "stand aside! Do you not know me? I am a Prætorian."

At that dreaded name the crowd quickly opened, and Marcellus passed through it. But scarcely had he moved five paces away than a voice exclaimed:

"Seize him! It is the Christian, Marcellus!"

A shout arose from the crowd. Marcellus needed no further warning. Dropping his load he started off down a side street toward the Tiber. The whole crowd pursued. It was a race for life and death. But Marcellus had been trained to every athletic sport, and increased the distance between himself and his pursuers. At last he reached the Tiber, and leaping in, he swam to the opposite side.

The pursuers reached the river's brink, but followed no farther.

CHAPTER X

THE ARREST

The trial of your faith worketh patience.

HONORIUS WAS SEATED in the chapel with one or two others, among whom was the Lady Cæcilia. The feeble rays of a single lamp but faintly illuminated the scene. They were silent and sad. A deeper melancholy than usual rested upon them. Around them was the sound of footsteps and of voices and a confused murmur of life.

Suddenly a quick step was heard, and Marcellus entered. The occupants of the chapel sprang up with cries of joy.

"Where is Pollio?" cried Cæcilia eagerly.

"I have not seen him," said Marcellus.

"Not seen him!" said Cæcilia, and she fell back upon her seat.

"Why? Is he beyond his time?"

"He ought to have returned six hours ago, and I am sick with anxiety."

"Oh, there is no danger," said Marcellus soothingly. "He can take care of himself." He tried to pass it off with a careless tone, but his looks belied his words.

"No danger!" said Cæcilia. "Alas, we know too well what new dangers there are. Never has it been so dangerous as now."

"What has delayed you, Marcellus? We had begun to give you up."

"I was stopped near the Via Alba," said Marcellus. "I dropped my load and ran to the river. The crowd followed, but I jumped into the river and swam across. There I took a circuitous route among the streets on the opposite side, after which I came across again and reached this place in safety."

"You had a narrow escape. A price is on your head."

"Have you heard it?"

"Yes, and much more. We have heard of the redoubled efforts which they are making to crush us. All through the day tidings of sorrow have been reaching us. We must rely more than ever on Him who alone can save us."

"We can baffle them still," said Marcellus hopefully.

"They watch our principal entrances," said Honorius.

"Then we can make new ones. The openings are numberless."

"They have offered rewards for all the prominent brethren."

"What then? We will guard those brethren more carefully than ever."

"Our means of living are gradually lessening."

"But there are as many bold and faithful hearts as ever. Who is afraid to risk his life now? There will never cease to be a supply of food so long as we live in the Catacombs. If we escape pursuit, we bring help to our brethren; if we die, we receive the crown of martyrdom."

"You are right, Marcellus. Your faith puts my fear to shame. How can those who live in the Catacombs be afraid of death? It is but a momentary gloom and it will pass. But this day we have heard much to distress our hearts and fill our spirits with dismay."

"Alas," continued Honorius in a mournful voice, "how are the people scattered and the assemblies left desolate! But a few months ago and there were fifty Christian assemblies within this city where the light of truth shone, and the sound of prayer and praise ascended to the Most High. Now they are overthrown, the people dispersed, and driven out of the sight of men."

He paused, overcome by emotion, and then in a low and plaintive voice he repeated the mournful words of the Eightieth Psalm:

How long wilt thou be angry against the prayer
  of thy people?
Thou feedest them with the bread of tears;
And givest them tears to drink in great measure.
Thou makest us a strife unto our neighbors;
And our enemies laugh among themselves.
Turn us again, O God of hosts,
And cause thy face to shine;
And we shall be saved.
Thou hast brought a vine out of Egypt:
Thou hast cast out the heathen, and planted it.
Thou preparedst room before it,

And didst cause it to take deep root,
And it filled the land.
The hills were covered with the shadow of it,
And the boughs thereof were like the goodly
    cedars.
She sent out her boughs to the sea,
And her branches unto the river.
Why hast thou broken down her hedges,
So that all who pass by the way do pluck her?
The boar out of the wood doth waste it,
And the wild beast of the field doth devour it.
Return, we beseech Thee, O God of hosts,
Look down from heaven, and behold, and visit
    this vine;
And the vineyard which thy right hand planted,
And the branch which thou madest strong for
    thyself.
It is burned with fire, it is cut down;
They perish at the rebuke of thy countenance.

"You are sad, Honorius," said Marcellus.
"Our sufferings, it is true, increase upon us; but
we can be more than conquerors through Him
who loved us. What says He?"

" 'To him that overcometh will I give to eat
of the tree of life, which is in the midst of the
paradise of God.'

" 'Be thou faithful unto death and I will give
thee a crown of life. He that overcometh shall
not be hurt of the second death.'

" 'To him that overcometh will I give to eat
of the hidden manna, and will give him a white
stone, and in the stone a new name written,
which no man knoweth saving he that received
it.'

" 'He that overcometh and keepeth my works unto the end, to him will I give power over the nations . . . and I will give him the morning star.'

" 'He that overcometh, the same shall be clothed in white raiment; and I will not blot his name out of the book of life, but I will confess his name before my Father, and before his angels.'

" 'Him that overcometh will I make a pillar in the temple of my God, and he shall go no more out: and I will write upon him the name of my God, and the name of the city of my God, which is new Jerusalem, which cometh down out of heaven from my God, and I will write upon him my new name.'

" 'To him that overcometh will I grant to sit with me on my throne, even as I also overcame, and am set down with my Father in his throne.' "

As Marcellus spoke these words, his form grew erect, his eye brightened, and his face flushed with enthusiasm. His emotions were transmitted to his companions, and as one by one these glorious promises fell upon their ears they forgot for a while their sorrows in the thought of their approaching blessedness. The New Jerusalem, the golden streets, the palms of glory, the song of the Lamb, the face of Him who sitteth upon the throne; all these were present to their minds.

"Marcellus," said Honorius, "you have driven away my gloom by your words; let us rise superior to earthly troubles. Come, brethren, lay aside your cares. The youngest born into the kingdom puts our faith to shame. Let us look to the joy set before us. 'For we know that if this earthly tabernacle were dissolved, we have a house not made with hands, eternal in the heavens.'

"Death comes nearer," he continued, "our enemies encircle us, and the circle grows narrower. Let us die like Christians."

"Why these gloomy forebodings?" said Marcellus. "Is death nearer to us than it was before? Are we not safe in the Catacombs?"

"Have you not heard, then?"

"What?"

"Of the death of Chrysippus?"

"Chrysippus! Dead! No! How? When?"

"The soldiers of the emperor were led down into the Catacombs by someone who knew the way. They advanced upon the room where service was going on. This was in the Catacombs beyond the Tiber. The brethren gave a hasty alarm and fled. But the venerable Chrysippus, either through extreme old age or else through desire for martyrdom, refused to flee. He threw himself upon his knees and raised his voice in prayer. Two faithful attendants remained with him. The soldiers rushed in, and even while Chrysippus was upon his knees they dashed out his brains. He fell dead at the first blow, and his two attendants were slain by his side."

"They have gone to join the noble army of martyrs. They have been faithful unto death, and will receive the crown of life," said Marcellus.

But now they were interrupted by a tumult without. Instantly everyone started upright.

"The soldiers!" exclaimed all.

But, no; it was not the soldiers. It was a Christian, a messenger from the world above. Pale and trembling, he flung himself upon the floor, and wringing his hands, cried out as he panted for breath:

"Alas! Alas!"

Upon the Lady Cæcilia the sight of this man produced a terrible effect. She staggered back against the wall trembling from head to foot, her hands clenched each other, her eyes stared wildly, her lips moved as though she wished to speak, but no sound escaped.

"Speak! Speak! Tell us all," cried Honorius.

"Pollio!" gasped the messenger.

"What of him?" said Marcellus sternly.

"He is arrested—he is in prison!"

At that intelligence a shriek burst forth which sounded fearfully amid the surrounding horrors. It came from the Lady Cæcilia. The next moment she fell heavily to the floor.

The bystanders hurried to attend her. They carried her away to her own quarters. There they applied the customary restoratives and she revived. But the blow had struck heavily, and though sense and feeling returned, yet she seemed like one in a dream.

Meanwhile the messenger had recovered strength, and told all that he knew.

"Pollio was with you; was he?" asked Marcellus.

"No, he was alone."

"On what errand?"

"Finding out the news. I was on one side of the street a little behind. He was coming home. We walked on until we came to a crowd of men. To my surprise, Pollio was stopped and questioned. I did not hear what passed, but I saw their threatening gestures, and at length saw them seize him. I could do nothing. I kept at a safe distance and watched. In about half an hour a troop of Prætorians came along. Pollio was handed over to them, and they carried him away."

"Prætorians?" said Marcellus. "Do you know the captain?"

"Yes; it was Lucullus."

"It is well," said Marcellus, and he fell into a deep fit of musing.

CHAPTER XI

THE OFFER

*Greater love hath no man than this, that a man
lay down his life for his friends.*

IT WAS EVENING in the Prætorian camp. Lucullus was in his room seated by a lamp which threw a bright light around. He was roused by a knock at the door. At once rising, he opened it. A man entered and advanced silently to the middle of the room. He then disencumbered himself of the folds of a large mantle in which he was dressed and faced Lucullus.

"Marcellus!" cried the other in amazement, and springing forward he embraced his visitor with every mark of joy.

"Dear friend," said he, "to what happy chance do I owe this meeting? I was just thinking of you, and wondering when we should meet again."

"Our meetings, I fear," said Marcellus sadly, "will not be very frequent now. I make this one at the risk of my life."

"True," said Lucullus, participating in the sadness of the other. "You are pursued, and there is a price on your head. Yet here you are

as safe as you ever were in those happy days before this madness seized you. O Marcellus, why
can they not return again?"

"I cannot change my nature nor undo what is
done. Moreover, Lucullus, although my lot may
appear to you a hard one, I never was so happy."

"Happy!" cried the other in deep surprise.

"Yes, Lucullus, though afflicted, I am not cast
down; though persecuted, I am not in despair."

"The persecution of the emperor is no slight
matter."

"I know it well. I see my brethren fall before
it every day. Every day the circle that surrounds
me is lessened. Friends leave me and never appear again. Companions go up to the city, but
when they return, they are carried back dead to
be deposited in their graves."

"And yet you say you can be happy?"

"Yes, Lucullus, I have a peace that the world
knows nothing of; a peace that cometh from
above, that passeth all understanding."

"I know, Marcellus, that you are too brave to
fear death; but I never knew that you had sufficient fortitude to endure calmly all that I know
you must now suffer. Your courage is super-
human, or rather it is the courage of madness."

"It comes from above, Lucullus. My Lord Jesus Christ is more to me than all the riches and
honor of the world. Once I was incapable of
feeling thus, but now old things have passed
away and all has become new. Sustained by this
new power, I can endure the utmost evils that
can be dealt upon me. I expect nothing but suf-

fering in life, and know that I shall die in agony; yet the thought cannot overcome the strong faith that is within me."

"It pains me," said Lucullus sadly, "to see you so determined. If I saw the slightest sign of wavering in you, I would hope that time might change or modify your feelings. But you seem to me to be fixed unalterably in your new course."

"God grant that I may remain steadfast unto the end!" said Marcellus fervently. "But it is not of my feelings that I came to speak. I come, Lucullus, to ask your assistance, to claim your sympathy and help. You promised me once to show me your friendship if I needed it. I come now to claim it."

"All that is in my power is yours already, Marcellus. Tell what you want."

"You have a prisoner."

"Yes, many."

"This is a boy."

"I believe my men captured a boy a short time since."

"This boy is too insignificant to merit capture. He is beneath the wrath of the emperor. He is yet in your power. I come, Lucullus, to implore his delivery."

"Alas, Marcellus, what is it that you ask? Have you forgotten the discipline of the Roman army, or the military oath? Do you not know that if I did this, I would violate that oath and make myself a traitor? If you asked me to fall upon my sword, I would do it more readily than this."

"I have not forgotten the military oath nor the discipline of the camp, Lucullus. I thought that this lad, being scarcely more than a child, might not be considered a prisoner. Do the commands of the emperor extend to children?"

"He makes no distinction of age. Have you not seen children as young as this lad suffer death in the Coliseum?"

"Alas, I have," said Marcellus, as his thoughts reverted to those young girls whose death-song once struck so painfully and so sweetly upon his heart. "This young boy, then, must also suffer?"

"Yes," said Lucullus, "unless he abjures Christianity."

"And that he will never do."

"Then he will rush upon his fate. The law does this, not I, Marcellus. I am but the instrument. Do not blame me."

"I do not blame you. I know well how strongly you are bound to obedience. If you hold your office, you must perform its duties. Yet let me make another proposal. Surrender of prisoners is not allowed, but an exchange is lawful."

"Yes."

"If I could tell you of a prisoner far more important than this boy, you would exchange, would you not?"

"But you have taken none of us prisoners."

"No, but we have power over our own peo-

ple. And there are some among us on whose
heads the emperor has placed a large reward.
For the capture of these a hundred lads like this
boy would be gladly given."

"Is it then a custom among Christians to betray one another?" asked Lucullus in surprise.

"No, but sometimes one Christian will offer
his own life to save that of another."

"Impossible!"

"It is so in this instance."

"Who is it that is offered for this boy?"

"I—Marcellus!"

At this astounding declaration Lucullus started
back.

"You!" he cried.

"Yes, I myself."

"You are jesting. It is impossible."

"I am serious. It is for this that I have already
exposed my life in coming to you. I have shown
the interest that I take in him by this great risk.
I will explain.

"This boy Pollio is the last of an ancient and
noble Roman family. He is the only son of his
mother. His father died in battle. He belongs to
the Servilii."

"The Servilii! Is his mother the Lady Cæcilia?"

"Yes. She is a refugee in the Catacombs. Her
whole life and love are wrapped up in this boy.
Every day she lets him go up into the city, a
dangerous adventure, and in his absence she suf-
fers indescribable agony. Yet she is afraid to

keep him there always for fear that the damp air which is so fatal to children may cut him off. So she exposes him to what she thinks is a smaller danger. This boy you have a prisoner. That mother has heard of it, and now lies hovering between life and death. If you destroy him she too will die, and one of the noblest and purest spirits in Rome will be no more.

"For these reasons I come to offer myself in exchange. What am I? I am alone in the world. No life is wrapped up in mine. No one depends on me for the present and the future. I fear not death. It may as well come now as at any other time. It must come sooner or later, and I would rather give my life as a ransom for a friend than lay it down uselessly.

"For these reasons, Lucullus, I implore you, by the sacred ties of friendship, by your pity, by your promise to me, give me your assistance now and take my life in exchange for his."

Lucullus rose to his feet and paced the room in great agitation.

"Why, O Marcellus," he cried at last, "do you try me so terribly?"

"My proposal is easy to receive."

"You forget that your life is precious to me."

"But think of this young lad."

"I pity him deeply. But do you think I can receive your life as a forfeit?"

"It is forfeited already, and will be surrendered sooner or later. I pray you let it be yielded up while it may be of service."

"You shall not die as long as I can prevent it. Your life is not yet forfeited. By the immortal gods, it will be long before you take your place in the arena."

"No one can save me when once I am taken. You might try your utmost. What could you do to save one on whom the emperor's wrath is falling?"

"I might do much to avert it. You do not know what might be done. But even if I could do nothing, still I would not listen to this proposal now."

"If I went to the emperor himself he would grant my prayer."

"He would take you prisoner at once and put both of you to death."

"I could send a messenger with my proposal."

"The message would never reach him; or at least not until it would be too late."

"There is then no hope?" said Marcellus mournfully.

"None."

"And you absolutely refuse to grant my request?"

"Alas, Marcellus, how can I be guilty of the death of my friend? You have no mercy on me. Forgive me if I refuse so unreasonable a proposal."

"The will of the Lord be done," said Marcellus. "I must hasten back. Alas, how can I carry with me this message of despair?"

The two friends embraced in silence, and

Marcellus departed, leaving Lucullus overcome with amazement at this proposal.

Marcellus returned to the Catacombs in safety. The brethren there who knew of his errand received him again with mournful joy.

The Lady Cæcilia still lay in a kind of stupor, only half-conscious of surrounding events. At times her mind would wander, and in her delirium she would talk of happy scenes in her early life. But the life which she had led in the Catacombs, the alternating hope and fear, joy and sorrow, the ever-present anxiety, and the oppressive air of the place itself had overcome both mind and body. Her delicate nature sank beneath the fury of such an ordeal, and this last heavy blow completed her prostration. She could not rally from its effects.

That night they watched around her couch. Every hour she grew feebler, and life was slowly but surely passing away. From that descent unto death not even the restoration of her son could have saved her.

But though earthly thoughts had left her and earthly feelings had grown faint, the one master passion of her later years held undiminished power over her. Her lips murmured still the sacred words which had so long been her support and consolation. The name of her darling boy was breathed from her lips though his present danger was forgotten; but it was the blessed name of Jesus that was uttered with the deepest fervor.

At length the end came. Starting from a long period of stillness, her eyes opened wide, a flush passed over her wan and emaciated face, and she uttered a faint cry, "Come, Lord Jesus!" With the cry life went out, and the pure spirit of the Lady Cæcilia had returned unto God who gave it.

CHAPTER XII

POLLIO'S TRIAL

Out of the mouths of babes and sucklings thou
hast ordained praise.

IT WAS A LARGE ROOM in a building not far
from the imperial palace. The pavement was
of polished marble, and columns of porphyry
supported a paneled dome. An altar with a
statue of a heathen deity was at one end of the
apartment. Magistrates in their robes occupied
raised seats on the opposite end. In front of
them were some soldiers guarding a prisoner.

The prisoner was the boy Pollio.

His face was pale, but his bearing was erect
and firm. The remarkable intelligence which
had always characterized him did not fail him
now. His quick eye took in everything. He knew
the inevitable doom that impended over him.
Yet there was no trace of fear or indecision
about him.

He knew that the only tie that bound him to
earth had been severed. Early that morning the
news of his mother's death had reached him. It
had been carried to him by a man who thought

129

that the knowledge of this would fortify his resolution. That man was Marcellus. The kindness of Lucullus had gained him an interview. His judgment had been correct. While his mother lived, the thought of her would have weakened his resolution; now that she was dead, he was eager to depart also. In his simple faith he believed that death would unite him at once to the dear mother whom he loved so fondly. With these feelings he awaited the examination.

"Who are you?"

"Marcus Servilius Pollio."

"What is your age?"

"Thirteen years."

At the mention of his name a murmur of compassion went around the assemblage, for that name was well-known in Rome.

"You are charged with the crime of being a Christian. What have you to say?"

"I am guilty of no crime," said the boy. "I am a Christian, and I am glad to be able to confess it before men."

"It is the same with them all," said one of the judges. "They all have the same formula."

"Do you know the nature of your crime?"

"I am guilty of no crime," said Pollio. "My faith teaches me to fear God and honor the emperor. I have obeyed every just law, and am not a traitor."

"To be a Christian is to be a traitor."

"I am a Christian, but I am not a traitor."

"The law of the State forbids you to be a Christian under pain of death. If you are a Christian, you must die."

"I am a Christian," repeated Pollio firmly.

"Then you must die."

"Be it so."

"Boy, do you know what it is to suffer death?"

"I have seen much of death during the last few months. I have always expected to lay down my life for my Lord when my turn should come."

"Boy, you are young. We pity your tender age and inexperience. You have been trained so peculiarly that you are scarcely responsible for your present folly. For all this we are willing to make allowance. This religion which infatuates you is foolishness. You believe that a poor Jew, who was executed two hundred years ago, is a God. Can anything be more absurd than this! Our religion is the religion of the State. It has enough in itself to satisfy the minds of young and old, ignorant and learned. Leave your foolish superstition and turn to our wiser and older religion."

"I cannot."

"You are the last of a noble family. The State recognizes the worth and the nobility of the Servilii. Your ancestors lived in pomp and wealth and power. You are a poor miserable boy and a prisoner. Be wise, Pollio. Think of the glory of your forefathers and throw aside the miserable obstacle that keeps you away from all their illustrious fame."

"I cannot."

"You have lived a miserable outcast. The poorest beggar in Rome fares better than you. His food is obtained with less labor and less humiliation. His shelter is in the light of day. Above all he is safe. His life is his own. He need not live in hourly fear of Roman justice. But you have had to drag out a wretched existence in want and danger and darkness. What has your boasted religion given you? What has this deified Jew done for you? Nothing; worse than nothing. Turn, then, from this deceiver. Wealth and comfort and friends and the honors of the State and the favor of the emperor will all be yours."

"I cannot."

"Your father was a loyal subject and a brave soldier. He died in battle for his country. He left you an infant, the heir of all his honors, and the last prop of his house. Little did he think of the treacherous influences that surrounded you to lead you astray. Your mother's mind, weakened by sorrow, surrendered to the insidious wiles of false teachers, and she again ignorantly wrought your ruin. Had your noble father lived you would now have been the hope of his ancient line; your mother, too, would have followed the faith of her illustrious ancestors. Do you value your father's memory? Has he no claims on your filial duty? Do you think it no sin to heap dishonor on the proud name that you bear, and throw so foul a blot upon the unsullied fame handed down to you from your fathers? Away with this delusion that blinds you. By your father's memory, by the honor of your family, turn from your present course."

"I can do them no dishonor. My faith is pure and holy. I can die, but I cannot be false to my Saviour."

"You see that we are merciful to you. Your name and your inexperience excites our pity. Were you but a common prisoner we would offer you in short words the choice between retraction or death. But we are willing to reason with you, for we do not wish to see a noble family become extinct through the ignorance or obstinacy of a degenerate heir."

"I thank you for your consideration," said Pollio; "but your arguments have no weight with me beside the higher claims of my Lord."

"Rash and thoughtless boy! There is another argument which you will find more powerful. The wrath of the emperor is terrible."

"Yet still more terrible is the wrath of the Lamb."

"You speak an unintelligible language. What is the wrath of the Lamb? You do not think of what is before you."

"My companions and friends have already endured all that you can inflict. I trust that I may have like fortitude."

"Can you endure the terrors of the arena?"

"I hope to have more than mortal strength."

"Can you face the savage lions and tigers that will then rush upon you?"

"He in whom I trust will not desert me in my time of need."

"You are confident."

"I confide in Him who loved me and gave Himself for me."

"Have you thought of the death by fire? Are you ready to meet the flames at the stake?"

"Alas! If I must bear it I will not shrink. At the worst it will soon be over, and then I shall be forever with the Lord."

"Fanaticism and superstition have taken complete possession of you. You know not what awaits you. It is easy to face threats, it is easy to utter words and make professions of courage. But how will it be with you when the dread reality comes upon you?"

"I will look to Him who never deserts His own in their hour of need."

"He has done nothing for you thus far!"

"He has done all for me. He gave His own life that I might live. Through Him I have received a nobler life than this which you take from me."

"This is but a dream of yours. How is it possible that a miserable Jew can do this?"

"He is the fullness of the Godhead; God manifest in the flesh. He suffered death of the body that we might receive life for the soul."

"Can nothing open your eyes? Is it not

enough that thus far your mad belief has brought you nothing but misery and woe? Must you still hold on to it? When you see that death is inevitable, will you not turn away from your errors?"

"He gives me strength to overcome death; I fear it not. I look upon death itself as but a change from this life of sorrow to an immortality of bliss. Whether I die by the wild beasts or by the flames, it will be all the same. He will enable me to continue faithful; He will support me and lead my spirit at once to immortal life in Heaven. The death with which you threaten me has no terrors; but the life to which you invite me is more terrible to me than a thousand deaths."

"For the last time we give you an opportunity. Rash youth, pause for one moment in your mad career of folly. Forget for an instant the insane counsels of your fanatical teachers. Think of all that has been said to you. Life is before you; life full of joy and pleasure; a life rich in every blessing. Honor, friends, wealth, power, all is yours. A noble name, and the possessions of your family, await you. They are all yours. To gain them you have but to take this goblet and pour the libation on yonder altar. Take it. It is but a simple act. Perform it quickly. Save yourself from a death of agony."

Every eye was fixed upon Pollio as this last offer was held out to him. Amazement had filled the minds of the spectators to find him thus far so unmoved. They could not account for it.

But even this last appeal had no effect. Pale but resolute, Pollio motioned away the proffered goblet.

"I will never be false to my Saviour."

At these words there was a moment's pause. Then the chief magistrate spoke:

"You have uttered your own doom. Away with him," he continued, addressing the soldiery.

CHAPTER XIII

THE DEATH OF POLLIO

*Be thou faithful unto death, and I will give thee a
crown of life.*

THE SENTENCE OF POLLIO was swift and
sure. On the following day there was a spectacle at the Coliseum. Crowded to its topmost
terrace of seats with the bloodthirsty Roman
multitude, it displayed the same sickening succession of horrors which has before been described.

Gladiators again fought and slew one another
singly and in multitudes. There was every different mode of combat known in the arena, and
of those the most deadly were sure to find the
most favor.

Again were the ever-recurring scenes of blood
and agony presented; the fierce champion of the
day received the short-lived congratulations of
the fickle spectators. Again man fought with
man, or waged a fiercer contest with the tiger.
Again the wounded gladiator looked up despair-
ingly for mercy, but saw only the signal of
death, the turned-down thumbs of the pitiless
spectators.

137

The satiated appetites of the multitude now demanded a larger supply of slaughter. The combats between men who were equally matched had lost their attraction for that day. It was known that Christians were reserved for the concluding spectacle, and the appearance of these was impatiently demanded.

Lucullus stood among the guards near the emperor's seat. Yet his brow was more thoughtful, and his former gaiety had all departed.

High up among the loftier seats behind him was a pale stern face that was conspicuous among all around it for the concentrated gaze which it fixed upon the arena. There was an expression of deep anxiety upon that face which made it far different from all within the vast enclosure.

Now the harsh sound of the gratings arose, and a tiger leaped forth into the arena. Throwing up its head and lashing its side with its tail, it stalked about glancing with fiery eyes upon the vast assemblage of human beings which hemmed it in.

Soon a murmur arose. A boy was thrust into the arena.

Pale in face and slight in limb, his slender form was nothing before the huge bulk of the furious beast. As if in derision, he was dressed like a gladiator.

Yet in spite of his youth and his weakness there was nothing in his face or manner that betrayed fear. His glance was calm and abstracted. He moved forward quietly to the center of the arena, and there, in the sight of all, he joined his hands together and lifted up his eyes and prayed.

Meanwhile, the tiger moved around as before. He had seen the boy, but the sight had no effect. He still raised his bloodshot eyes toward the lofty walls and occasionally uttered a savage growl.

The man with the stern sad face looked on with all his soul absorbed in that gaze.

There appeared to be no desire on the part of the tiger to attack the boy, who still continued praying.

The multitude now grew impatient. Murmurs arose and cries and shouts with the intention of maddening the tiger and urging him on.

But now, even in the midst of the tumult, there came forth the sound of a voice deep and terrible:

How long, O Lord, holy and true, dost thou not avenge our blood on them that dwell upon the earth?

A deep stillness followed. Everyone in surprise looked at his neighbor.

But the silence was soon broken by the same voice, which rang out in terrific emphasis:

Behold, he cometh with clouds;
And every eye shall see him,
And they also which pierced him:
And all kindreds of the earth shall wail because
of him.
Even so, Amen.

* * *

Thou art righteous, O Lord,
Which art, and wast, and shalt be,
Because thou hast judged thus.
For they have shed the blood of saints and
    prophets,
And thou hast given them blood to drink;
For they are worthy.
Even so, Lord God Almighty,
True and righteous are thy judgments!

But now murmurs and cries and shouts passed around. Soon the cause of the disturbance became known.

"It is an accursed Christian"—"It is the fanatic Cinna"—"He has been confined four days without food"—"Bring him out"—"Throw him to the tiger!"

Shouts and execrations arose on high and mingled in one vast roar. The tiger leaped around in frenzy. The keepers within heard the words of the multitude and hurried to obey.

Soon the gratings opened. The victim was thrust in. Fearfully emaciated and ghastly pale, he tottered forward with tremulous steps. His eyes had an unearthly luster, his cheeks a burning flush, and his neglected hair and long beard were matted in a tangled mass.

The tiger saw him, and came leaping toward him. Then at a little distance away the furious beast crouched. The boy arose from his knees and looked. But Cinna saw no tiger. He fixed his eyes on the multitude, and waving his withered arm on high he shouted in the same tone of menace:

"Woe! woe! woe to the inhabitants of the earth—"

His voice was hushed in blood. There was a leap, a fall, and all was over.

And now the tiger turned toward the boy. His thirst for blood was fully aroused; with bristling hair, flaming eyes, and sweeping tail he stood facing his prey.

The boy saw that the end was coming, and again fell upon his knees. The crowd was hushed to stillness, and awaited in deep excitement the new scene of slaughter. The man who had been gazing so intently now rose upward and stood erect, still watching the scene below. Loud cries arose from behind him which increased still louder, "Down!" "Down!" "Sit down!" "You obstruct the view!"

But the man either did not hear or else purposely disregarded. At length the crowd grew so noisy that the officers below turned to see the cause.

Lucullus was one of them. Turning round he saw the whole scene. He started and grew pale as death.

"Marcellus!" he cried. For a moment he staggered back, but soon recovering he hurried away to the scene of the disturbance.

But now a deep murmur broke forth from the multitude. The tiger, who had been walking round and round the boy, lashing himself to greater fury, now crouched for a spring.

The boy arose. A seraphic expression was upon his face. His eyes beamed with a lofty enthusiasm. He saw no longer the arena, the high surrounding walls, the far-extending seats with innumerable faces; he saw no more the relentless eyes of the cruel spectators, or the gigantic form of his savage enemy.

Already his soaring spirit seemed to enter into the golden gates of the New Jerusalem, and the ineffable glory of the noonday of Heaven gleamed upon his sight.

"Mother, I come to thee! Lord Jesus, receive my spirit!"

His words sounded clearly and sweetly upon the ears of the multitude. They ceased, and the tiger sprang. The next moment there was nothing but a struggling mass half-hidden in clouds of dust.

The struggle ended. The tiger started back, the sand was red with blood, and upon it lay the mangled form of the truehearted, the noble Pollio.

Then amid the silence that followed there came forth a shout that sounded like a trumpet peal and startled everyone in the assembly:

"O death, where is thy sting? O grave, where is thy victory? . . . Thanks be to God who giveth us the victory through our Lord Jesus Christ."

A thousand men rose with a simultaneous burst of rage and indignation. Ten thousand hands were outstretched toward the bold intruder.

"A Christian!"—"A Christian!"—"To the

flames with him!"—"Throw him to the tiger!"
—"Hurl him into the arena!"

Such were the shouts that answered the cry.

Lucullus reached the spot just in time to res-
cue Marcellus from a crowd of infuriated Romans, who were about to tear him in pieces. The
tiger below was not fiercer, more bloodthirsty
than they. Lucullus rushed among them, dash-
ing them to the right and left as a keeper among
wild beasts.

Overawed by his authority, they fell back, and
soldiers approached.

Lucullus gave Marcellus in charge to them,
and led the company out of the amphitheater.

Outside he took charge of the prisoner himself. The soldiers followed them.

"Alas, Marcellus! Was it well to throw away
your life?"

"I spoke from the impulse of the moment.
That dear boy whom I loved died before my
eyes! I could not restrain myself. Yet I do not
repent. I, too, am ready to lay down my life for
my King and my God."

"I cannot reason with you. You are beyond
the reach of argument."

"I did not intend to betray myself, but since
it is done I am content. Nay, I am glad, and I
rejoice that it is my lot to suffer for my Redeemer."

"Alas, my friend! Have you no regard for
life?"

"I love my Saviour better than life."

"See, Marcellus, the road before us is open. You can run quickly. Flee, and be saved."

Lucullus spoke this in a hurried whisper. The soldiers were some twenty paces behind. The chances were all in favor of escape.

Marcellus pressed the hand of his friend.

"No, Lucullus. I would not gain life by your dishonor. I love the warm heart that prompted it, but you shall not be led into difficulty by your friendship for me."

Lucullus sighed, and walked on in silence.

CHAPTER XIV

THE TEMPTATION

All this will I give thee if thou wilt fall down and worship me.

THAT NIGHT Lucullus remained in the cell with his friend. He sought by every possible argument to shake his resolution. He appealed to every motive that commonly influences men. He left no means of persuasion unused. All in vain. The faith of Marcellus was too firmly fixed. It was founded on the Rock of Ages, and neither the storm of violent threats nor the tenderer influences of friendship could weaken his determination.

"No," said he, "my course is taken and my choice is made. Come weal, come woe, I must follow it out to the end. I know all that is before me. I have weighed all the consequences of my action, but in spite of all I will continue as I have begun."

"It is but a small thing that I ask," said Lucullus. "I do not wish you to give up this religion forever, but only for the present. A terrible persecution is now raging, and before its fury all must fall, whether young or old, high or low.

You have seen that no class or age is respected. Pollio would have been saved if it had been possible. There was a strong sympathy in his favor. He was young, and scarcely accountable for his errors; he was also noble, the last of an ancient family. But the law was inexorable, and he suffered its penalty. Cinna, too, might have been overlooked. He was neither more nor less than a madman. But so vehement is the zeal against Christians that even his evident madness was no security whatever for him."

"I know it well. The Prince of darkness struggles against the assembly of God, but it is founded on a Rock, and the gates of Hell cannot prevail against it. Have I not seen the good, the pure, the noble, the holy, and the innocent all suffer alike? Do I not know that there is no mercy for the Christian? I knew it well long ago. I have always been prepared for the consequences since I have known Jesus Christ as my Lord and Saviour."

"Hear me, Marcellus. I have said that I asked but a small thing. This religion which you prize so highly need not be given up. Keep it, if it must be so. But make allowance for circumstances. Since the storm is raging bow before it. Take the course of a wise man, not of a fanatic."

"What is it that you would have me to do?"

"It is this. In the course of a few years a change will take place. Either the persecution will wear itself out, or a reaction will take place, or the emperor may die and other rulers with dif-

ferent feelings may succeed. It will then be safe
to be a Christian. Then these people who are
now afflicted may come back from their hiding
places to occupy their old places, and to rise to
dignity and wealth. Remember this. Do not
therefore throw away a life which yet may be
serviceable to the State and happy to yourself.
Cherish it for your own sake. Look about you
now. Consider all these things. Lay aside your
religion for a time, and return to that of the
State. It need only be for a time. Thus you may
escape from present danger, and when happier
times return, you may go back and be a Christian again."

"This is impossible, Lucullus. It is abhorrent
to my soul. What, can I thus be doubly a hypo-
crite? If you knew what has taken place in me,
you could not ask me to perjure my immortal
soul to the world and to my God. Better to die at
once by the severest tortures that can be in-
flicted."

"You take such extreme views that I despair
of saving you. Will you not look at this subject
rationally? It is not perjury but policy; not
hypocrisy but wisdom."

"God forbid that I should do this thing and
sin against Him!"

"Look further also. You will not only benefit
yourself but others. These Christians whom you
love will be assisted by you far more than they
are now. In their present situation you know
well that they are enabled to live by the sympathy and assistance of those who profess the

religion of the State but in secret prefer the religion of the Christians. Do you call these men hypocrites and perjurers? Are they not rather your benefactors and friends?"

"These men have never learned the Christian's faith and hope as I have. They have never known the new birth, the new divine nature, the abiding presence of the Holy Spirit, communion with the Son of the living God, as I now know. They have not known the love of God springing up within their hearts to give them new feelings and hopes and desires. For them to sympathize with the Christians and to help them is a good thing; but the *Christian* who could be base enough to abjure his faith and deny the Saviour that redeemed him, could never have enough generosity in his traitorous soul to assist his forsaken brethren."

"Then, Marcellus, I have but one more offer to make, and I go. It is a last hope. I do not know whether it will be possible or not. I will try it, however, if I can but gain your consent. It is this. You need not abjure your faith; you need not sacrifice to the gods; you need not do anything whatever of which you disapprove. Let the past be forgotten. Return again, not in heart, but in outward appearance, to what you were before. You were then a gay, lighthearted soldier, devoted to your duties. You never took part in any religious services. You were seldom present in the temples. You passed your time in the camp, and your devotions were in private. You gathered your instruction from the books of the philosophers and not from the priests. Be all this again. Return to your duties.

"Appear again in public in company with me; again join in pleasant conversation, and devote yourself to your old pursuits. This will be easy and pleasant to do and it will not require anything that is base or distasteful. The authorities will overlook your absence and your misconduct, and if they are not willing that you should be restored to all your former honors, then you can be placed in your former command in your old legion. All will then be well. A little discretion will be needed, a wise silence, an apparent return to your former round of duties. If you remain in Rome it will be thought that the tidings of your conversion to Christianity was wrong; if you go abroad it will not be known."

"No, Lucullus, even if I would consent, the plan which you propose would not be possible for many reasons. Proclamations have been made about me, rewards have been offered for my apprehension, and above all, my last appearance in the Coliseum before the emperor himself was sufficient to take away all hope of pardon. But I could not consent. My Saviour cannot be worshiped in this way. His followers must confess Him openly. 'Whosoever,' He says, 'shall confess me before men, shall the Son of man also confess him before the angels of God.' To deny Him in my life or in outward appearance is precisely the same as denying Him by the formal manner which the law lays down. This I cannot do. I love Him who first loved me and gave Himself for me. My highest joy is to proclaim Him before men; to die for Him will be my noblest act, and the martyr's crown my most glorious reward."

Lucullus said no more, for he found that all persuasion was useless. The remainder of the time was passed in conversation about other things. Marcellus did not waste these last precious hours which he passed with his friend. Filled with gratitude for his noble and generous affection, he sought to recompense him by making him acquainted with the highest treasure that man can possess—the faith of Christ.

Lucullus listened to him patiently, more through friendship than interest. Yet some, at least, of Marcellus' words were impressed upon his memory.

On the following day the trial took place. It was short and formal. Marcellus was immovable, and received his condemnation with a calm demeanor. The afternoon of the same day was the time appointed for him to suffer. He was to die, not by the wild beasts, nor by the hand of the gladiator, but by the keener torments of death by fire.

It was in that place where so many Christians had already borne their witness to the truth that Marcellus sealed his faith with his life. The stake was placed in the center of the Coliseum, and the faggots were heaped high around it.

Marcellus entered, led on by the brutal keepers, who added blows and ridicule to the horrors of the approaching punishment. He looked around upon the vast circle of faces, both of men and women, hard, cruel, and pitiless; he looked upon the arena and thought of the thousands of Christians who had preceded him in suffering, and had gone from thence to join the noble army of martyrs who will worship forever around the throne. He thought of the children whose death he had witnessed, and recalled once more their triumphant song:

> Unto Him that loved us,
> To Him that washed us from our sins.

Now the keepers seized him rudely and led him to the stake, where they bound him with strong chains so that escape was impossible.

" 'I am now ready to be offered,' " murmured he, " 'and the time of my departure is at hand. . . . Henceforth there is laid up for me a crown of righteousness, which the Lord, the righteous judge, shall give me at that day.' "

Now the torch was applied, and the flames rose up and dense volumes of smoke concealed the martyr for a while from view. When it passed away he was seen again standing amid the fire with upturned face and clasped hands.

The flames increased around him. Nearer and nearer they came, devouring the faggots and enveloping him in a circle of fire. Now they threw over him a black veil of smoke, again they dashed forward and licked him with their forked tongues.

But the martyr stood erect, calm amid suffering, serene amid his dreadful agony, by faith cleaving to his Saviour. He was there, though they saw Him not; His everlasting arm was round about His faithful follower, and His Spirit inspired him.

Nearer grew the flames and yet nearer. Life, assailed more violently, trembled in her citadel, and the spirit prepared to wing its way to its paradise of rest.

At last the sufferer gave a convulsive start, as though some sharper pang flashed resistlessly through him. But he conquered his pain with a violent effort. Then he raised his arms on high and feebly waved them. Then, with a last effort of expiring nature, he cried out in a loud voice, "Victory!"

With the cry life seemed to depart, for he fell forward amid the rushing flames, and the spirit of Marcellus had "departed to be with Christ, which is far, far better."

CHAPTER XV

LUCULLUS

The memory of the just is blessed.

At the scene of torture and of death there was one spectator whose face, full of agony, was never turned away from Marcellus; whose eyes saw every act and expression, whose ears drank in every word. Long after all had departed he remained in the same place, the only human being in all the vast extent of deserted seats. At length he rose to go.

The old elasticity of his step had departed. He moved with a slow and feeble gait; his abstracted gaze and expression of pain made him look like a man suddenly struck with disease. He motioned to some of the keepers, who opened for him the gates that led to the arena.

"Bring me a cinerary urn," said he, and he walked forward to the dying embers.

A few fragments of crumbled bone, pulverized by the violence of the flames, were all that remained of Marcellus.

Silently Lucullus took the urn which the keeper brought him, and collecting what human

153

fragments he could find, he carried away the dust.

As he was leaving he was accosted by an old man. He stopped mechanically.

"What do you wish of me?" said he courteously.

"I am Honorius, an elder among the Christians. A dear friend of mine was put to death this day in this place. I have come to see if I could obtain his ashes."

"It is well that you have addressed yourself to me, venerable man," said Lucullus. "Had you proclaimed your name to others you would have been seized, for there is a price on your head. But I cannot grant your request. Marcellus is dead, and his ashes are here in this urn. They will be deposited in the tomb of my family with the highest ceremonies, for he was my dearest friend, and his loss makes the earth a blank to me and life a burden."

"You, then," said Honorius, "can be no other than Lucullus, of whom I have so often heard him speak in words of affection?"

"I am he. Never were there two friends more faithful than we. If it had been possible I would have saved him. He would never have been arrested had he not thrown himself into the hands of the law. O hard fate! At a time when I had made arrangements that he should never be arrested, he came before the emperor himself, and I was compelled with my own hands to lead him whom I loved to prison and to death."

"What is your loss is to him immeasurable

gain. He has entered into the possession of immortal happiness."

"His death was a triumph," said Lucullus. "The death of Christians I have noticed before, but never have I been so struck by their hope and confidence. Marcellus died as though death were an unspeakable blessing."

"It was so to him, but not more so than to many others who lie buried in the gloomy place where we are forced to dwell. To their numbers I wish to add the remains of Marcellus. Would you be willing to part with them?"

"I had hoped, venerable Honorius, that since my dear friend had left me I might have at least the mournful pleasure of giving to his remains the last pious honors, and of weeping at his tomb."

"But, noble Lucullus, would not your friend have preferred a burial with the simple ceremonies of his new faith, and a resting place among those martyrs with whose names his is now associated forever?"

Lucullus was silent, and thought for some time. At length he spoke:

"Of his wishes there can be no doubt. I will respect them, and deny myself the honor of performing the funereal rites. Take them, Honorius. But I will, nevertheless, assist at your services. Will you permit the soldier, whom you only know as your enemy, to enter your retreat and to witness your acts?"

"You shall be welcome, noble Lucullus, even as Marcellus was welcome before you, and perhaps you will receive among us the same blessing that was granted to him."

"Do not hope for anything like that," said Lucullus. "I am far different from Marcellus in taste and feeling. I might learn to feel kindly toward you, or even to admire you, but never to join you."

"Come with us, then, whatever you are, and be present at the funeral services of your friend. A messenger will come for you tomorrow."

Lucullus signified his assent, and after handing over the precious urn to the care of Honorius, he went sadly to his own home.

On the following day he went with the messenger to the Catacombs. There he saw the Christian community, and beheld the place of their abode. But from the previous accounts of his friend he had gained a clear idea of their life, their sufferings, and their afflictions.

Again the mournful wail arose in the dim vaults and echoed along the arched passageways, that wail that spoke of a new brother committed to the grave; *but the grief that spoke of mortal sorrow was succeeded by a loftier strain that expressed the faith of the aspiring soul, and a hope full of desire for their beloved Lord.*

Honorius took the precious scroll, the Word of life, whose promises were so powerful to sustain amid the heaviest burden of grief, and in solemn tones read that part of I Corinthians which in every age and in every clime has been so dear to the heart that looked beyond the realms of time to seek for comfort in the prospect of the resurrection.

Then he raised his head and in fervent tones offered up a prayer to the Holy One of Heaven, through Christ the divine Mediator, by whom death and the grave had been conquered and eternal life secured.

The pale, sad face of Lucullus was conspicuous among the mourners. If he was not a Christian, he could still admire such glorious doctrines and listen with awe to such exalted hopes. It was he who placed the loved ashes within their final resting place; he, whose eyes took the last look at the dear remains; and he whose hands lifted to its place the slab whereon the name and the epitaph of Marcellus was engraved.

Lucullus went to his home, but he was a changed man. The gaiety of his nature seemed to have been driven out by the severe afflictions that he had endured.

He had rightly said that he would not become a Christian. The death of his friend had filled him with sadness, *but there was no sorrow for sin, no repentance, no desire for a knowledge of the true and living God*. He had lost the power of taking pleasure in the world, but had gained no other source of happiness.

Yet the memory of his friend produced one effect on him. He felt a sympathy for the poor and oppressed people with whom Marcellus had associated. He admired their constancy and pitied their unmerited sufferings. He saw that all the virtue and goodness left in Rome were in the possession of these poor outcasts.

These feelings led him to give them assistance. He transferred to them the friendship and the promise of aid which he had once given to Marcellus. His soldiers arrested no more, or if they did arrest any they were sure to escape in some way. His high position, vast wealth, and boundless influence were all at the service of the Christians. His palace was well known to them as their surest place of refuge or assistance, and his name was honored as that of their most powerful human friend.

But all things have an end; and so the constant sufferings of the Christians and the friendship of Lucullus at length were brought to a termination. In about a year after the death of Marcellus the stern Emperor Decius was overthrown,[1] and a new ruler entered into the imperial power. The persecution was stayed. Peace returned to the assemblies, and the Christians came forth from the Catacombs again to dwell in the glad light of day, again to sound in the ears of men the praises of Him who had redeemed them, and again to carry on their never-ending contest with the hosts of evil.

Years passed on, but no change came to Lucullus. When Honorius came from the Catacombs he was taken by Lucullus to his own palace, and maintained there for the rest of his life. He sought to repay his debt of gratitude to his noble benefactor by making him acquainted

[1] See Note, Page 19.

with the truth, but he died without seeing his desires gratified.

The blessing came at last, but not till years had passed away. Far on beyond the prime of manhood, even upon the borders of old age, the Saviour found Lucullus. For years the world had lost all charms. Wealth and honor and power were nothing to him; his life was tinged with sadness that nothing could cure. But the Spirit of God at length laid hold of him, and through His divine power he at last was enabled to rejoice in the love of that Saviour, of whose power over the human heart he had witnessed so many striking proofs.

Many centuries have rolled over the city of the Cæsars since the persecution of Decius drove the humble followers of Jesus into the gloomy Catacombs. Let us take our stand upon the Appian Way and look around.

Before us goes the long array of tombs up to the ancient city. Here the mighty men of Rome once found a resting place, carrying with them even to their graves all the pomp of wealth, of glory, and of power. Beneath our feet are the rude graves of those whom in life they cast out as unworthy to breathe the same air of Heaven.

Now what a change! Around us lie these stately tombs all in ruins, their sanctity desecrated, their doors broken down, their dust scattered to the winds. The names of most of those who were buried here are unknown; the empire which they reared has fallen; the legions which they led to conquer have slept the sleep that knows no waking until the second resurrection.

But on the memory of the persecuted ones who rest below, the assembly of God on earth looks back adoring; their sepulcher has become a place of pilgrimage; and the work in which they took such a noble part has been handed down to us to be continued until Jesus comes.

Humbled, despised, outcast, afflicted, fame may not have written their names upon the scroll of history, yet this much we know, their names are written in the Book of Life, and their fellowship will be with those of whom it is written:

These are they which came out of the great tribulation,
And have washed their robes,
And made them white in the blood of the Lamb.
Therefore are they before the throne of God,
And serve him day and night in his temple.
And he that sitteth on the throne shall dwell among them.
They shall hunger no more, neither thirst any more,
Neither shall the sun light on them, nor any heat.
For the Lamb which is in the midst of the throne shall feed them,
And shall lead them unto living fountains of waters:
And God shall wipe away all tears from their eyes.

THE END